THE
MOON ERA

By
JACK WILLIAMSON

I0541413

ARMCHAIR FICTION
PO Box 4369, Medford, Oregon 97504

HE PLUNGED BACK IN TIME TO WHEN THE MOON WAS YOUNG

Stephen Conway was a typical, run-of-the-mill high school teacher. He coached the school football team. He led a comfortable but uneventful life. Everything seemed safe, nondescript, but safe.

Then one day he was summoned to the home of his uncle, Enfield Conway, a man he had never met, a man of extreme wealth and power. During that meeting Stephen Conway was given the most extraordinary opportunity ever bequeathed from one man to another—the chance to become the first human being to travel into the depths of outer space. His destination—the moon! His uncle's revolutionary new spacecraft was nearly complete. And in return for this adventure, Stephen was to be given a life of wealth and luxury. But there was just one gnawing question: would he be able to come back…alive?

FOR A SECOND COMPLETE NOVEL, TURN TO PAGE 95

CAST OF CHARACTERS

STEPHEN CONWAY
His life was lackluster, but then one day he was offered a chance at millions. All he had to do was travel to the moon and back!

ENFIELD CONWAY
This eccentric millionaire dreamt of one day constructing a great ship that would carry man into space. His first target…the moon.

THE MOTHER
She was the sole survivor of a great Lunar race, but within her were the seeds to a new race—if only she could survive.

THE ETERNAL ONES
They were no longer normal living creatures. All that was left of them were their brains—encased within mechanical bodies.

MULLER
This scientist was the first to admit that the Lunar spaceship he had constructed had little chance of bringing a man back alive.

GORTON
He helped instruct Stephen Conway on how to pilot his uncle's moonship—a venture he was sure would bring certain death!

CHAPTER ONE
The Beginning

WE WERE seated at dinner in the long dining room of my uncle's Long Island mansion. There was glistening silver plate, and the meal had been served with a formality to which I was unaccustomed. I was ill at ease, though my uncle and I sat alone at the table. The business of eating, without committing an egregious blunder before the several servants, took all my attention.

It was the first time I had ever seen my uncle, Enfield Conway. A tall man, stiffly erect, dressed severely in black. His face, though lean, was not emaciated as is usual at his age of seventy years. His hair, though almost perfectly white, was abundant, parted on the side. His eyes were blue, and strong; he wore no glasses.

A uniformed chauffeur had met me at the station in the afternoon. The butler had sent an entirely unnecessary valet to my luxurious room. I had not met my uncle until he came down to the dining room.

"I suppose, Stephen, you are wondering why I sent for you," he said in his precise manner, when the servants had carried away the last course, leaving cigars, and a bottle of mineral water for him.

I nodded. I had been instructor of history in a small high school in Texas, where his telegram had reached me. There had been no explanation, merely a summons to Long Island.

"You are aware that some of my patents have been quite profitable."

Again I nodded. "The evidence surrounds me."

"Stephen, my fortune amounts to upwards of three and a half million. How should you like to be my heir?"

"Why, sir—I should not refuse. I'd like very much to be."

"You can, if you wish, earn that fortune. And fifty thousand a year while I live."

I pushed back the chair and rose to my feet in excitement. Such riches were beyond my dreams! I felt myself trembling.

"Anything—" I stammered. "I'll do anything you say, to earn that. It means—"

"Wait," he said, looking at me calmly. "You don't know yet what I require. Don't commit yourself too soon."

"What is it?" I asked in a quivering voice.

"Stephen, I have been working in my private laboratory here for eleven years. I have been building a machine. The best of my brains have gone into that machine. Hundreds of thousands of dollars. The efforts of able engineers and skilled mechanics.

"Now the machine is finished. It is to be tested. The engineers who worked with me refused to try the machine. They insist that it is very dangerous.

"And I am too old to make the trial. It will take a young man, with strength, endurance, and courage.

"You are young, Stephen. You look vigorous enough. I suppose your health is good? A sound heart? That's the main thing."

"I think so," I told him. "I've been coaching the Midland football team. And it isn't many years since I was playing college football, myself."

"And you have no dependents?"

"None. But what is this machine?"

"I will show you. Come."

He rose, agilely enough for one of his seventy years, and led the way from the long room. Through several magnificent rooms of the big house. Out into the wide, landscaped grounds, beautiful and still in the moonlight.

I followed silently. My brain was confusion. A whirl of mad thought. All this wealth whose evidence surrounded me might be my own! I cared nothing for luxury, for money itself. But the fortune would mean freedom from the thankless toil of pedagogy. Books. Travel. Why I could see with my own eyes the scenes of history's dramatic moments! Finance research expeditions of my own! Delve with my own hands for the secrets of Egypt's sands, uncover the age-old enigmas of ruined mounds that once were proud cities of the East!

We approached a rough building—resembling an airplane hangar—of galvanized iron, which glistened like silver in the rays of the full moon.

Without speaking, Uncle Enfield produced a key from his pocket, unlocked the heavy padlock on the door. He entered the building, switching on electric lights inside it.

"Come in," he said. "Here it is. I'll explain it as well as I can."

I WALKED through the narrow doorway and uttered an involuntary exclamation of surprise at sight of the huge machine that rested upon the clean concrete floor.

Two huge disks of copper, with a cylinder of bright, chromium-plated metal between them. Its shape vaguely suggested that of an ordinary spool of adhesive plaster, from which a little has been used—the polished cylinder, which was of smaller diameter than the disks, took the place of the roll of plaster.

The lower of the massive disks rested on the concrete floor. Its diameter was about twenty feet. The cylinder above it was about sixteen feet in diameter, and eight feet high. The copper disk above was the same size as the lower one.

Small round windows stared from the riveted metal plates forming the cylinder. The whole was like a building, it burst on me. A circular room with bright metal walls. Copper floor and copper roof projecting beyond those walls.

My uncle walked to the other side of this astounding mechanism. He turned a projecting knob. An oval door, four feet high, swung inward in the curving wall. Four inches thick. Of plated steel. Fitting very tightly against cushions of rubber.

My uncle climbed through the door, into the dark interior. I followed with a growing sense of wonder and excitement. I groped toward him through the darkness. Then I heard the click of a switch, and lights flashed on within the round chamber.

I gazed about me in astonishment.

Walls, floor, and ceiling were covered with soft, white fiber. The little room was crowded with apparatus. Clamped against one white wall was a row of the tall steel flasks in which commercial oxygen is compressed. Across the room was a bank of storage batteries. The walls were hung with numerous instruments, all clamped neatly in place. Sextants. Compasses. Pressure gauges. Numerous dials whose functions were not apparent. Cooking utensils. An automatic pistol. Cameras. Telescopes. Binoculars.

In the center of the room stood a table or cabinet, with switches, dials, and levers upon its top. A heavy cable, apparently of aluminum, ran from it to the ceiling.

I was gazing about in bewilderment. "I don't understand all this—" I began.

"Naturally," said my uncle. "It is quite a novel invention. Even the engineers who built it did not understand it. I confess that the theory of it is yet beyond me. But what happens is quite simple.

"Eleven years ago, Steven, I discovered a new phenomenon. I had happened to charge two parallel copper plates, whose distances apart had a certain very definite relation to their combined masses, with a high tension current at a certain frequency.

"The plates, Stephen, were in some way—how, I do not pretend to understand—cut out of the Earth's gravitational field. Insulated from gravity. The effect extended to any object placed between them. By a slight variation of the current's strength, I was able to increase the repulsion, until the plates pulled upward with a force approximately equal to their own weight.

"My efforts to discover the reason for this phenomenon—it is referred to in my notes as the Conway Effect—have not been successful. But I have built this machine to make a practical application of it. Now that it is finished, the four engineers who helped design it have deserted. They refused to assist with any trials."

"Why?" I asked.

"Muller, who had the construction in charge, somehow came to the conclusion that the suspension or reversal of gravity was due to motion in a fourth dimension. He claimed that he had experimental proof of his theory, by building models of the device, setting the dials, and causing them to vanish. I would have none of it. But the other men seemed to accept his ideas. At any rate, they refused with him to have any part in the tests. They thought they would vanish, like Muller says his models did, and not come back."

"The thing is supposed to rise above the ground?" I asked.

"Quite so." My uncle smiled. "When the force of gravitation is merely suspended, it should fly off the Earth at a tangent, due to the diurnal rotation. This initial velocity, which in these latitudes amounts to considerably less than one thousand miles per hour, can be built up at will, by reversing gravitation, and falling away from the Earth."

Falling away from the Earth!" I was staggered. "And where is one to fall."

"This machine was designed for a trip to the moon. At the beginning of the voyage, gravitation will be merely cut out, allowing the machine to fly off on a tangent, toward the point of intersection with the moon's orbit. Safely beyond the atmosphere, repulsion can be used to build up the acceleration. Within the gravitational sphere of the moon, positive gravitation can be utilized further to increase the speed. And reversed gravitation to retard the velocity, to make possible a safe landing. The return will be made in the same manner."

I was staring at him blankly. A trip to the moon seemed insane, beyond reason. Especially for a professor of history, with only a modicum of scientific knowledge. And it must be dangerous, if those engineers... But three million—what dangers would I not face for such a fortune?

"Everything has been done," he went on, "to insure the comfort and safety of the passenger. The walls are insulated with a fiber composition especially worked out to afford protection from the cold of space, and from the unshielded radiation of the sun. The steel armor is strong enough not only to hold the necessary air pressure, but also to stop any ordinary meteoric particles.

"You notice the oxygen cylinders, for maintaining that essential element in the air. There is automatic apparatus for purifying it. It is pumped through caustic soda to absorb the carbon dioxide, and through refrigerator tubes to condense the excess moisture.

"The batteries, besides energizing the plates, are amply powerful to supply lights and heat for cooking.

"That, I believe, fairly outlines the machine and the projected voyage. Now it is up to you. Take time to consider it fully. Ask me any questions you wish."

HE SAT down deliberately in the large, cushioned chair, beside the central table, which was evidently intended for the operator. He stared at me alertly, with calm blue eyes.

I was extremely agitated. My knees had a weak feeling, so that I desired to sit down also, though I was so nervous that I kept striding back and forth across the resilient white fiber of the floor.

Three million! It would mean so much! Books, magazines, maps—I should have to economize no longer. Years—all my life, if I wished—abroad. The tombs of Egypt. The sand-covered cities of the Gobi. My theory that mankind originated in South Africa. All those puzzles that I had longed to be able to study. Stonehenge! Angkor! Easter Island!

But the adventure seemed madness. A voyage to the moon! In a craft condemned by the very engineers that had built it. To be hurled away from the Earth at speeds no man had attained before. To face unknown perils of space. Dangers beyond guessing. Hurtling meteors. The all-penetrating cosmic rays. The burning heat of the sun. The absolute zero. What, beyond speculation and theory, did men know of space? I was no astronomer; how was I to cope with the emergencies that might rise?

"How long will it take?" I demanded suddenly.

My uncle smiled a little. "Glad you are taking it seriously," he said. "The duration of the voyage depends on the speed you make, of course. A week each way is a conservative estimate. And perhaps two or three days on the moon. To take notes. Photograph it. Move around a little, if possible, land in several different places. There is oxygen and concentrated food to last six months. But a fortnight should see you nearly back. I'll go over the charts and calculations with you."

"Can I leave the machine once I'm on the moon?"

"No. No atmosphere. And it would be too hot in the day, too cold at night. Of course an insulated suit and oxygen mask might be devised. Something like diving armor. But I haven't worked at that. You will be expected just to take a few pictures, be prepared to describe what you have seen."

I continued to pace the floor, pausing sometimes to examine some piece of apparatus. How would it feel, I wondered, to be shut up in here? Drifting in space. Far from the world of my birth. Alone. In silence. Entombed. Would it not drive me mad?

My uncle rose suddenly from the chair.

"Sleep on it, Stephen," he advised. "See how you feel in the morning. Or take longer if you wish."

He switched off the light in the machine and led the way out into the shed. And from it into the brilliant moonlight that flooded the wide, magnificent grounds about the great house that would be one of the prizes of this mad adventure.

As he was locking the shed, I gazed up at the moon.

Broad, bright disk. Silvery, mottled. Extinguishing the stars with argent splendor. And all at once it came over me—the desire to penetrate the enigmatic mystery of this companion world that men have watched since the race began.

What an adventure? To be the first human to tread this silver planet. To be the first to solve its age-old riddles. Why think of Angkor, or Stonehenge, of Luxor and Karnak, when I might win the secrets of the moon?

Even if death came, what did it matter against the call of this adventure? Many men would trade their lives eagerly for such a chance.

Suddenly I was strong. All weakness had left me. All fear and doubt. A few moments before I had been tired, wishing to sit down. Now vast energy filled me. I was conscious of an extraordinary elation. Swiftly I turned to my uncle.

"Let's go back," I said. "Show me as much about it as you can tonight. I am going."

He gripped my hand tightly, without a word, before he turned back to the lock.

CHAPTER TWO
Toward the Moon

IT WAS in the second week, after that sudden decision came to me, that I started. At the end my uncle became a little alarmed and tried to persuade me to stay longer, to make more elaborate preparations. I believe that he was secretly becoming fond of me, despite his brisk precise manner. I think he took the opinion of his engineers seriously enough to consider my return very uncertain.

But I could see no reason for longer delay. The operation of the machine was simple; he had explained it quite fully.

There was a switch to close, to send current from the batteries through the coils that raised it to the potential necessary to energize the copper disks. And a large rheostat that controlled the force, from a slight decrease in gravity, to a complete reversal.

The auxiliary apparatus, for control of temperature and atmosphere, was largely automatic. And not beyond my limited mechanical comprehension. I was certain that I should be able to make any necessary repairs or adjustments.

Now I was filled with the greatest haste to undertake the adventure. No doubt or hesitation had troubled me since the moment of the decision. I felt only a longing to be sweeping away from the Earth. To view scenes that the ages had kept hidden from human eyes; to tread the world that has always been the symbol of the unattainable.

My uncle recalled one of the engineers, a sallow young fellow named Gorton. On the second morning, to supplement my uncle's instruction he went over the machine again, showing me the function of every part. Before he left, he warned me.

"If you are idiot enough to get in that darned contraption, and turn on the power," he told me, "you'll never come back. Muller said so. And he proved it. So long as the batteries and coil are outside the field of force between the plates, the plates act according to schedule, and rise up in the air.

"But Muller made self-contained models. With the battery and all inside. And they didn't rise up. They went out! Vanished. Just like that!" He snapped his fingers.

"Muller said the things moved along another dimension, right out of our world. And he ought to know. String of degrees a mile long. Into another dimension. No telling what sort of hell you'll blunder into."

I thanked the man. But his warnings only increased my eagerness. I was about to tear aside the veil of the unknown. What if I did blunder into new worlds? Might they not yield rewards of knowledge richer than those of the barren moon? I might be a new Columbus, a greater Balboa.

I slept a few hours in the afternoon, after Gorton had gone. I felt no conscious need of slumber, but my uncle insisted upon it. And to my surprise, I fell soundly asleep, almost as soon as I lay down.

At sunset, we went down again to the shed in which the machine was housed. My uncle started a motor, which opened the roof like a pair of enormous doors, by means of pulleys and cables. The red light of the evening sky streamed down upon the machine.

We made a final inspection of all the apparatus. My uncle explained again the charts and instruments that I was to use in navigating space. Finally he questioned me for an hour, making me explain the various parts of the machine, correcting any error.

I was not to start until nearly midnight.

We returned to the house, where an elaborate dinner was waiting. I ate almost absently, hardly noticing the servant, of whom I had been so conscious upon my arrival. My uncle was full of conversation. Talking of his own life, and asking me many questions about my own, and about my father, whom he had seen last when they were boys. My mind was upon the adventure before me—I could answer him only disjointedly. But I was aware that he had taken a real liking for me; I was not surprised at his request that I postpone the departure.

At last we went back down to the machine. The white moon was high; its soft radiance bathed the gleaming machine through the opened roof. I stared up at its bright disk. Was it possible that in a short week I should be there, looking back upon the Earth? It seemed madness! But the madness of glorious adventure!

Without hesitation, I clambered through the oval door. A last time my uncle wrung my hand. He had tears in his eyes. And his voice was a little husky.

"I want you to come back, Stephen."

I swung the door into its cushioned seat, upon massive hinges, tightened the screws that were to hold it. A final glance about the white-walled interior of the machine. All was in order. The chronometer by the wall, ticking steadily, told me that the moment had come.

My uncle's anxious face was pressed against one of the ports. I smiled at him. Waved. His hand moved across the port. He left the shed.

I dropped into the big chair beside the table, reached for the switch. With my fingers upon the button, I hesitated the merest second. Was there anything else? Anything neglected? Anything I had yet to do on Earth? Was I ready to die, if so I must?

The deep, vibrant hum of the coils, beneath the table, answered the pressure of my finger. I took the handle of the rheostat, swung it to the zero mark, where gravitation was to be cut off completely.

My sensation was exactly as if the chair and the floor had fallen from under me. The same sensation that one feels when an elevator drops very abruptly. I almost floated out of the chair. I had to grasp at the arm of it to stay within it.

For a few moments I experienced nauseating vertigo. The white crowded room seemed to spin about me. To drop away endlessly beneath me. Sick, helpless, miserable, I clung weakly to the great chair. Falling. Falling...falling. Would I never strike bottom?

THEN I realized, with relief, that the sensation was due merely to the absence of gravity's familiar pull. The machine had worked! My last, lingering doubt was killed. Strange elation filled me.

I was flying away from the Earth. Flying.

The thought seemed to work a miracle of change in my feelings. The dreadful, dizzy nausea gave way to a feeling of exhilaration—of lightness. I was filled with a sense of power and well being, such as I had never before experienced.

I left the great chair, floated rather than walked to one of the windows.

Already I was high in the air. So high that the moon-lit Earth was a dim and misty plain before me. I could see many lights; the westward sky was aglow above New York. But already I was unable to pick out the lights at my uncle's mansion.

The machine had risen through the opened roof of the shed. It was driving out into space, as it had been planned to do! The adventure was succeeding.

As I watched, the Earth sank visibly, became a great concave bowl of misty silver. Expanded slowly, as the minutes went by. And became suddenly convex. A huge dark sphere washed with pale gray light.

Presently, after an hour, when the dials showed that I was beyond the faintest trace of atmosphere, I returned to the table and increased the power, moving the rheostat to the last contact. I looked at charts and chronometer. According to my uncle's calculations, four hours at this acceleration were required before the controls were set again.

I returned to the window and stared in amazement at the Earth, that I had left vast and silver gray and motionless.

It was spinning madly, backward!

The continents seemed to race beneath me. I was now high enough to see a vast section of the globe: Asia, North America, Europe, Asia again—in seconds.

It was madness! The Earth spinning in a few moments, instead of the usual twenty-four hours. And turning backward! But I could not doubt my eyes. Even as I watched, the planet seemed to spin faster. Ever faster! The continental outlines merged into dim indistinctness.

I looked away from the mad Earth in bewilderment. The firmament was very black. And the very stars were creeping about it, with visible motions!

Then the sun came into view, plunging across the sky like a flaming comet. It swung supernally across my field of vision, then vanished. Appeared again. And again. Its motion became ever swifter.

What was the meaning of such an apparent revolution of the sun about the sky? It meant, I knew, that Earth and moon had swung about the star. That a year had passed! But were years going by as fast as my chronometer ticked off the seconds?

Another strange thing—I could recognize the constellations of the Zodiac, through which the sun was plunging. And it was going backward! As the Earth was spinning backward!

I moved to another window, searched for the moon, my goal. It hung still among spinning stars. But in its light there was a flicker, far more rapid than the flashing of the sun across the wild heavens. I wondered, then knew that I saw the waxing and waning of the moon. Months, passing so swiftly that soon the flicker became a gray blur.

The flashing past of the sun became more frequent, until it was a strange belt of flame about the strange heavens, in which the stars crept and moved like living things.

A universe gone mad! Suns and planets spinning helpless in the might of a cosmic storm! The machine from which I watched the only sane thing in a runaway cosmos!

Then reason came to my rescue.

Earth, moon, sun, and stars could not all be mad. The trouble was with *myself!* My perceptions had changed. The machine—

Slowly it came to me, until I knew I had grasped the truth.

Time, true time, is measured by the movements of the heavenly bodies. Our day is the time of Earth's rotation on its axis. Our year the period of its revolution about the sun.

Those intervals had become crowded so thick in my perception that they were indistinguishable. Then countless years were spinning past, while I hung still in space!

Incredible! But the conclusion was inevitable.

And the apparent motion of Earth and sun had been backward.

That meant—and the thought was staggering—that the ages were reeling backward. That I was plunging at an incalculable rate into the past.

Vaguely I recalled magazine articles that I had read about the nature of space and time. A lecture. The subject had fascinated me, though I had only a layman's knowledge of it.

The lecturer had defined our universe in terms of space-time. A four-dimensional "continuum," time was a fourth dimension, he had said. An extension as real as the three of what we call space, and not completely distinguishable from them. A direction in which motion would carry one into the past, or into the future.

All memory, he had said, is a groping back along this dimension, at right angles to teach of the three of space. Dreams, vivid memories, he insisted, carry one's consciousness in reality back along this dimension, until the body, swept relentlessly along the stream of time, drags it forward again.

THEN I recalled what my uncle had told me of the refusal of his engineers to try the machine. Recalled Gorton's warning. Muller, they both had told me, had declared that the machine would move along a fourth dimension, out of our world. He had made models of the machine and they had vanished when the power was turned on.

Now I knew that Muller was right. His models had vanished because they had been carried into the past. Had not continued to exist in the present time.

And now I was moving along that fourth dimension. The dimension of time. And very swiftly, for the years went past too fast for counting.

The reversal of gravitation, it came to me, must be some effect of this change of direction in time. But I am not a scientist. I can explain the "Conway Effect" no better than my uncle, for all the wonders that it has brought into my life.

At first it was horribly strange and terrifying.

After I had thought out my explanation of the mad antics of the Earth and sun and moon, and of the hurrying stars, I was, however, no longer frightened. I gazed out through my small round ports at the melting firmament with some degree of equanimity.

I continued to watch the charts my uncle had prepared, and to make adjustments of the rheostat when they were indicated by the chronometer.

And presently, feeling hungry, I toasted biscuits on the electric stove, cut off a generous slice of a cheese that I found in the supplies, opened a vacuum bottle of steaming chocolate, and made a hearty and very satisfactory meal.

When I had finished, the aspect of the space about me was unchanged. Crawling stars, already forming themselves into constellations, the most of which were unfamiliar. The sun a broad belt of burning gold, counting off the years too swiftly for the eye to follow. A living flame that girdled the firmament. The Earth was a huge gray sphere, spinning so swiftly behind me that no detail was visible.

And even the moon, hanging in space ahead, was turning slowly. No longer was the same familiar face toward me, and toward the Earth. Already I had reached a point in past time at which the moon was tuning on its axis more rapidly than it revolved about the Earth. The tidal drag had not yet completely stopped the moon's apparent rotation.

And if already the moon was turning, what would it be when I reached it? Hurtling into the past as I was, would I see oceans cover its dry sea floors? Would I see an atmosphere soften the harsh outlines of its rugged mountains? Would I see life, vegetation, spread over its plains? Was I to witness the rejuvenation of an aged world?

It seemed fantastic. But it was taking place. The speed of rotation slowly increased as I watched.

The hours slipped past.

I became heavy with sleep. The two days before the departure had not been easy. I had worked day and night to familiarize myself with the machine's operation. The nervous strain had been exhausting. The amazing incidents of the voyage had kept me tense, sapped my strength.

The chart told me that no change was to be made in the controls for many hours. I inspected the gauges, which showed the condition of the atmosphere in the chamber. Oxygen content, humidity, temperature, were correct. The air smelled sweet and clean. I completed the rounds, found everything in order.

I adjusted the big chair to a reclining position, and threw myself upon it. For hours I slept, waking at intervals to make a tour of inspection.

Sometimes, in the following days, I wondered if I should be able to go back. Muller's models had carried no operator, of course, to start them on the flight back through time to the starting point. Would I be able to reverse the time-flight? If I followed the directions on the operating chart on the flight back, would I be flung forward through the ages, back to my own era?

I wondered. But the speculation brought forth no conclusion. A strange, unique experience was mine. Glorious adventure. Death was not too high a price to pay.

It did not even occur to me to attempt to turn back toward the Earthward when I found that I was slipping through time. And I did not have sufficient control of the machine to have done so, had I even wished. Dependent upon the chart for navigating instructions, I could not have plotted an accurate return path from the midway point. And I knew no way to stop my flight, except by using the repulsion of the moon's reversed gravitation.

My flight lasted six days, by the chronometer.

Long before the end, the moon was spinning very swiftly. And the edges of its outline had become hazy, so that I knew it had an atmosphere.

I followed the charted directions until I was in the upper-most layers of that atmosphere. The moon's surface was sliding very rapidly beneath me, and the atmosphere with it, due to the swift rotation of the satellite. Consequently, fierce winds screamed about the machine.

I hung in the atmosphere, merely using enough power to balance the moon's comparatively feeble gravitational pull, until the pressure of that rushing wind swept me with it. The mistily indistinct surface slowed and became motionless beneath me.

With power decreased still further, I settled slowly, watching alertly through the ports.

A towering, crimson mountain loomed above the mists below. I dropped toward it, increasing the power a little. At last I hovered motionless above a narrow, irregular plateau, near the peak, that seemed covered with soft scarlet moss.

Slowly I cut down the power. With hardly a shock, the machine settled in the moss.

I was on the moon! The first of my race to set foot upon an alien planet! What adventures might await me?

CHAPTER THREE
When the Moon Was Young

WITH the power cut off entirely, I ran to the ports. There had been no time to scan my surroundings during the uncertainties of the landing. Now I peered out eagerly.

The moonscape was as strange a sight as man had ever seen.

The machine had come down in thick green moss, which looked soft as a Persian rug. A foot deep it was. Dark green fibers closely intertwined. In an unbroken carpet it covered the sloping plateau upon which I had landed, and extended almost to the top of the rugged peak to northward.

To the south and west lay a great valley, almost level, miles across. Beyond it rose a dim range of green hills, rugged summits bare and black. A broad river, glinting white in the distance, flowed down the valley, from northwest, into the south. Then there must be an ocean in that direction.

Strange jungle covered that valley, below the green moss of the mountains. Masses of green. Walls of yellow lining the wide smooth river. Dense forests of gigantic plants, weirdly and grotesquely strange. They grew more luxuriant, taller, than similar plants could upon the Earth, because a much feebler gravitation opposed their growth.

Equaly strange was the sky.

Darker than on Earth, perhaps because the atmosphere was thinner. A deep, pure, living blue. A blue that was almost violet. No cloud marred its liquid azure splendor.

The sun hung in the glorious eastward sky. Larger than I had known it, Whiter. A supernal sphere of pure white flame.

Low in the west was an amazing disk. A huge ball of white, a globe of milky light. Many times the diameter of the sun. I wondered at it. And realized that it was—the Earth! The Earth young as Venus had been in my time. And like Venus, shrouded in white clouds never broken. Were the rocks still glowing beneath those clouds, I wondered? Or had the life begun—the life of my farthest progenitors?

Would I ever see my native land again, upon that resplendent, cloud-hidden planet? Would the machine carry me back into the future, when I attempted return? Or would it hurl me farther into the past, to plunge flaming into the newborn and incandescent world?

That question I put resolutely from my mind. A new world was before me. A globe strange and unexplored. Why worry about return to the old?

My eyes went back to the broad valley below me, along the banks of the broad river, beneath the majestic range of green mountains. Clumps of gold, resembling distant groves of yellow trees. Patches of green looked like meadows of grass. Queer, puzzling uprights of black.

I saw things moving. Little bright objects, that rose and fell slightly as they flew. Birds? Gigantic insects? Or creatures stranger than either?

Then I saw the balloons. Captive balloons, floating above the jungles of the valley. At first I saw only two, hanging side by side, swaying a little. Then three more, beyond. Then I distinguished dozens, scores of them, scattered all over the valley.

I strained my eyes at them. Were there intelligent beings here, who had invented the balloons? But what would be the object of hanging them about above the jungles, by the hundred.

I remembered the powerful prism binoculars hanging on the wall beside me. I seized them, focused them hurriedly. The weird jungle leaped toward me in the lenses.

The things were doubtless balloons. Huge spheres of purple, very bright in the sunlight. Anchored with long red cables. Some of them, I estimated, were thirty feet in diameter. Some, much smaller. I could make out no baskets. But there seemed to be small dark masses upon their lower sides, to which the red ropes were attached.

I left them and surveyed the jungle again.

A mass of the yellow vegetation filled the lenses. A dense tangle of slender yellow stems, armed with terrible rows of long, bayonet-like thorns. A thick tangle of sharp yellow thorns, it seemed, with no more stalk than was necessary to support them against the moon's feeble pull. A wall of cruel spikes, impenetrable.

I found a patch of green. A mass of soft, feathery foliage. A sort of creeper, it seemed, covering rocks, and other vegetation—though it did not mingle with the yellow scrub. Enormous, brilliantly white, bell-shaped blooms were open upon it here and there.

A flying thing darted across my vision. It looked like a gigantic moth, frail wings dusted with silver.

Then I made out a little cluster of curious plants. Black, smooth, upright stalks, devoid of leaf or branch. The tallest looked a foot in diameter, a score in height. It was crowned with a gorgeous red bloom. I noticed that no other vegetation grew near any of them. About each was a little cleared circle. Had they been cultivated?

Hours went by as I stared out through the ports, at this fascinating and bewildering moonscape.

Finally I recalled the pictures that my uncle had requested me to take. For two or three hours I was busy with the cameras. I made exposures in all directions, with ordinary and telescopic lenses. I photographed the scene with color filters. And finally I made motion pictures, swinging the camera to take a panoramic view.

It was almost sunset when I had finished. It seemed strange that the day was passing so swiftly, until I looked at the chronometer and found that it was not keeping pace with the sun. I decided that the period of rotation must be rather less than twenty-four hours. I later found it to be about eighteen hours, divided into days and nights of very nearly equal length.

DARKNESS came very swiftly after sunset, due to the comparatively small size and quick rotation of the moon. The stars burst out splendidly through the clear air, burning in constellations utterly strange.

A heavy dew was soon obscuring the ports. As I later discovered, clouds almost never formed in this light atmosphere. Nearly the entire precipitation was in the form of dew, which was amazingly abundant. The tiny droplets on the glass were soon running in streams.

After a few hours, a huge and glorious snow-white sphere rose in the east. The Earth. Wondrous in size and brilliance. The weird jungle was visible in its silvery radiance almost as in daylight.

Suddenly I realized that I was tired, and very sleepy. The anxiety and prolonged nervous strain of the landing had been exhausting. I threw myself down upon the reclining chair and fell into immediate oblivion.

The white sun was high when I woke. I found myself refreshed—keenly hungry. And conscious of a great need for physical exercise. Accustomed to an active life, I had been shut up in that little round room for seven days. I felt that I must move about and breathe fresh air.

Could I leave the machine?

My uncle had told me that it would be impossible because of lack of atmosphere. But there was plainly air about me, on this young moon. Would it be breathable?

I pondered the question. The moon, I knew, was formed of materials thrown off from the cooling Earth. Then should its atmosphere not contain the same elements as that of Earth?

I decided to try it. Open the door slightly, and sniff experimentally. Close it immediately if there seemed anything wrong.

I loosened the screws that held the heavy door and tried to pull it open. It seemed fastened immovably. In vain I tugged at it, looked to see if I had left a screw, or if something was amiss with the hinges. It refused to budge.

For minutes I was baffled. The explanation came to me suddenly. The pressure of the atmosphere outside was much less than that within the machine. Since the door opened inward, it was the unbalanced pressure upon it that held it.

I found the valve that was to be opened to free the chamber of any dangerous excess of oxygen that might escape, and spun it open. The air hissed out noisily.

I sat down in the chair to wait. At first I felt no symptoms of the lessening pressure. Then I was conscious of a sensation of lightness, of exhilaration. I noticed that I was breathing faster. My temples throbbed. For a few minutes I felt a dull ache in my lungs.

But the sensations did not become unduly alarming, and I left the valve open. The hissing sound gradually decreased, and finally died away completely.

I rose and went to the door, feeling a painful short-ness of the breath as I moved. The heavy door came open quite easily now. I sniffed the air outside. It bore a strange, heavy, unfamiliar fragrance that must have been carried from the jungle in the valley. And I found it oddly stimulating—it must have been richer in oxygen than the air in the machine.

With the door flung wide, I breathed deeply of it.

At first I had thought merely of strolling up and down for a while, in the moss outside the machine. But now I decided, quite suddenly, to hike to the lower edge of the green-carpeted plateau, perhaps a mile away, and look at the edge of the jungle.

I looked about for equipment that I should take and got together a few items: a light camera in case I should see something worth taking; the binoculars; a vacuum bottle full of water, and a little food so that I should not have to hasten back to eat.

And finally I took down the automatic pistol on the wall, a .45 Colt. It must have been included with the machine's equipment merely as a way of merciful escape, in case some failure made life in the little round compartment unendurable. There was only one box of ammunition. Fifty cartridges. I loaded the weapon, and slipped the remainder into my pocket.

Gathering up the other articles, I scrambled through the oval door, and stood upon the rim of the lower copper disk, drawing the door to behind me, and fastening it.

And stepped off, upon the moon.

The thick, fibrous moss yielded under my foot, surprisingly. I stumbled, fell into its soft green pile, and in scrambling to my feet, I forgot the lesser gravity of the moon, threw myself into the air, tumbling once more into the yielding moss.

In a few minutes I had mastered the art of walking under the new conditions, so that I could stride along with some confidence, going clear of the ground at every step, as if I had worn seven league boots. Once I essayed a leap, it carried me twenty feet into the air, and twice as far forward. It seemed that I hung in the air an unconscionable time, and floated down very slowly. But I was helpless, aloft, sprawling about, unable to get my feet beneath me. I came down on my shoulder, and it would have been painfully bruised had it not been for the thick moss.

I realized that my strength upon the moon was quite out of proportion to my weight. I had muscles developed to handle a mass of 180 pounds. Here my weight was only 30 pounds. It would be some time, I supposed, before I could learn the exact force required to produce the result desired. Actually, I found myself adapted to these new conditions in a surprisingly short space of time.

FOR a time I was conscious of shortness of breath, especially after violent exertion. But soon I was accustomed to the lighter air as well as the lesser gravitation.

In half an hour I had arrived at the edge of the reel plateau. A steep slope fell before me to the edge of the jungle, perhaps two-thirds of a mile farther below. A slope carpeted with the thick fiber of the green moss.

It was a weird scene: clear cerulean sky, darkly, richly blue; the huge white globe of the hot Earth setting beyond the farther range of green mountains, and the wide valley with the broad silvery stream, winding among golden forests and patches of green. Then there were the purple balloons floating here and yon, huge spheres swaying on the red cables that anchored them above the jungle.

I seated myself on the moss, where I could overlook that valley of eldritch wonder. I remained there for some time, staring out across it while I ate most of the food that I had brought, and half-emptied the bottle of water.

Then I decided to descend to the edge of the jungle.

The sun was just at the meridian—the whole of the short afternoon, four hours and a half, was yet before me. I had ample time, I thought, to go down the slope to the edge of the jungle and return before the sudden nightfall.

I had no fear of getting lost. The glittering armor of the machine was visible over the whole plateau. And the jagged triple peak to the northward of it was a landmark that should be visible over the whole region. There should be no difficulty about return.

Nor, while I realized that the jungle might hide hostile life, did I fear attack. I intended to be cautious, and not to penetrate beyond the edge of the jungle. I had the automatic, which I was sure gave me greater power of destruction than any other animal on the planet. Finally in case of difficulty, I could rely upon the superior strength of my muscles, which must be far stronger, in proportion to my weight, than those of native creatures.

I found progress easy on the long, mossy incline. My skill at traveling under lunar conditions of gravity was increasing with practice. I found a way of moving by deliberate, measured leaps, each carrying me twenty feet or more.

In a few minutes I found myself approaching the edge of the jungle. But that was not so sharp a line as it had appeared from above. The first vegetation other than the moss was scattered clumps of a plant resembling the cactus of my native Southwest.

Thick, fleshy disks growing one upon another, edge to edge. They were not green, however, but of a curious pink, flesh-like color. They bore no thorns, but were studded with little black protuberances, or knobs, of doubtful function. The plants I first approached were small and appeared stunted. The lower clumps seemed large and more thickly spaced.

I paused to examine one. I walked around it slowly, curiously. Photographed it from several angles. Then I ventured to touch it with my foot. Several of the little black knobs broke—they proved to be thin-walled vesicles containing a black liquid. My nose perked, and then an overpowering and extremely unpleasant odor assailed me. I retreated hastily.

A hundred yards farther on I came upon the green creepers. Thick stems coiled like endless serpents over the ground, with innumerable fronds rising from them, terminating in feathery sprays of green. Here and there were huge white blooms, nearly six feet across, resembling great bells of burnished silver. From them, evidently, came the heavy perfume that I had noticed upon opening the door of the machine.

The creepers formed an unbroken mass of vibrant green, several feet deep. It probably would have been impossible to penetrate it without damaging or crushing the delicate foliage. I decided to go no farther in that direction. The creeper might have such means of protection as the malodorous sacs of the fleshy plants above. Or dangerous creatures, counterparts of terrene snakes, might lie concealed beneath the dense foliage.

For some distance I followed along the edge of the mass of creepers, pausing at intervals to make photographs. I was approaching a thicket or forest of the yellow scrub. A wall of inch-thick stems, each armed at intervals of a few inches with dagger-like thorns, all interwoven. A hundred feet high, I estimated. Interlaced so closely that a rat would have had difficulty in moving through it without impaling himself upon a needle-sharp spike.

Then I paused to watch one of the purple balloons, which seemed swaying in my direction, increasing the length of the red anchor-cable that held it to the jungle behind. A strange thing, that huge purple sphere, tugging at the thin scarlet cable that held it. Tugging almost like a thing alive, I thought.

Several times I photographed it, but its distance was so great that I feared none of the images would be satisfactory. It seemed to be moving toward me, perhaps carried by some breeze that did not reach the ground. I thought perhaps it would soon be near enough for a good picture.

CHAPTER FOUR
The Balloon Menace

I STUDIED it closely, trying to see if it had an intelligent pilot or occupant. But I was unable to settle the point. There was certainly no basket. But black arms or levers seemed to project in a cluster, from its lowest part, to manipulate the cables.

Nearly an hour I waited, watching it. It moved much closer during that time; until, in fact, it was almost directly overhead, and only a few hundred feet high. The red cable slanted from it back into the jungle. It seemed to be loose, dragging.

At last I got a picture that satisfied me. I decided to go on and examine the tangle of yellow thorn-brush or scrub at closer range.

I had taken my eyes from the purple balloon, and turned to walk away, when it struck.

A red rope whipped about me.

The first I knew, it was already about my shoulders. Its end seemed to be weighted, for it whirled about my body several times, wrapping me in sticky coils.

The cable was about half an inch in diameter and made of many smaller crimson strands, fastened together with the adhesive stuff that covered it. I recall its appearance very vividly, even the odd, pungent, disagreeable odor of it.

Half a dozen coils of the red cable had whipped about me before I realized that anything was amiss. Then it tightened suddenly, dragging me across the red moss upon which I had been standing. Toward the edge of the jungle.

Looking up in horror, I saw that the rope had been thrown from the purple balloon I had been watching. Now the black arms that I had seen were working swiftly, coiling it up again—with me caught neatly on the end.

The great sphere was drawn down a little, as my weight came upon it. It seemed to swell. Then, having been dragged along until I was directly beneath it, I was lifted clear of the ground.

I was filled with unutterable terror. I was panting, my heart was beating swiftly, and I felt endowed with terrific strength. Furiously I writhed in my gluey bonds, struggled with the strength of desperation to break the red strands.

But the web had been spun to hold just such frightened, struggling animals as myself. It did not break.

Back and forth I swung over the jungle, like a pendulum. With a constantly quickening arc! For the cable was being drawn up. Once more I looked upward, and saw a sight to freeze me in dreadful stupefaction of horror.

The whole balloon was a living thing!

I saw its two black and terrible eyes, aflame with hot evil, staring at me from many bright facets. The black limbs I had seen were its legs, growing in a cluster at the bottom of its body—now furiously busy coiling up the cable that it had spun, spider-like, to catch me. I saw long jaws waiting, black and hideously fanged, drooling foul saliva. And a rapier-thin pointed snout, that must be meant for piercing and sucking body juices.

The huge purple sphere was a thin-walled, muscular sac, which must have been filled with some light gas, probably hydrogen, generated in the body of the creature. The amazing being floated above the jungle, out of harm's way, riding free on the wind, or anchored with its red web, lassoing its prey and hauling it up to feast hideously in the air.

For a moment I was petrified, dazed and helpless with the new horror of that thin snout, with black-fanged jaws behind it.

Then fear bred superhuman strength in me. I got my arms free, dragging them from beneath the sticky coils. I reached above my head, seized the red cable in both hands, and tried to break it between them.

It refused to part, despite my fiercest efforts.

Only then did I recall the pistol in my pocket. If I could reach it in time, I might be able to kill the monster. And the gas should escape through the riddled sac, letting me back to the surface. I was already so high that the fall would have been dangerous, had I succeeded in my desperate effort to break the web.

The viscid stuff on the cable clung to my hands. It took all my strength to tear them loose. But at last they were free, and I fumbled desperately for the gun.

A red strand was across the pocket in which I had the weapon. I tore at it. It required every ounce of my strength to slip it upward. And it adhered to my fingers again. I wrenched them loose, snatched out the automatic. It touched the gluey rope, stuck fast. I dragged it free, moved the safety catch with sticky fingers, raised it above my head.

Though it had been seconds only since I was snatched up, already I had been lifted midway to the dreadful living balloon. I glanced downward. The distance was appalling. I noticed that the balloon was still drifting, so that I hung over a thicket of the yellow scrub.

Then I began shooting at the monster. It was difficult to aim, because of the regular jerks as the ugly black limbs hauled on the cable. I held the gun with both hands and fired deliberately, very carefully.

The first shot seemed to have no effect.

At that second, I heard a shrill, deafening scream. And I saw that one of the black limbs was hanging limp.

I shot at the black, many-faceted eyes. Though I had no knowledge of the creature's anatomy, I supposed that its highest nervous centers should be near them.

THE third shot hit one of them. A great blob of transparent jelly burst through the faceted surface, hung pendulous. The thing screamed horribly again. The black arms worked furiously, hauling me up.

I felt a violent upward jerk, stronger than the regular pulls that had been raising me. In a moment I saw the reason. The creature had released the long anchor cable, which had held it to the jungle. We were plunging upward. The moon was spinning away below.

The next shot seemed to take no effect. But at the fifth, the black limbs twitched convulsively. I am sure that the creature died almost at once. The limbs ceased to haul upon the cable, hung still. But I fired the two cartridges remaining in the gun.

That was the beginning of a mad aerial voyage.

The balloon shot upward, when the anchor cable was dropped. And after it was dead, the muscular sac seemed to relax, expand, so that it rose still faster.

Within a few minutes I must have been two miles above the surface. A vast area was visible beneath me; the convexity of the moon's surface, which, of course, is much greater than that of the Earth's, was quite apparent.

The great valley lay below, between the green mountain ranges. Splotched with blue and yellow. The white river twisting along it, wide and silvery. I could see into other misty valleys beyond the green ranges, and on the curving horizon were more hills, dim and black in the distance.

The plateau upon which I had landed was like a green-covered table, many thousands of feet below. I could distinguish upon it a tiny bright disk, which I knew was the machine that I had left so unwisely.

Though there had been little wind at the surface, it seemed that I rose into a stratum of air, which was moving quite rapidly into the northwest. I was carried swiftly along; the floor of the great valley glided back beneath me. In a few minutes the machine was lost to view.

I was, of course, rendered desperate at being swept away from the machine. I kept myself oriented, and tried to watch the landmarks that passed beneath me. It was fortunate, I thought, that the wind was driving me up the valley, instead of across the red ranges. I might be able to return to the machine by following down the great river, until the triple peak, near which I had left the machine. Despair came over me, however, at the realization that I was not likely to be able to traverse so vast a stretch of the unknown jungles of this world, without my ignorance of its perils leading me into some fatal blunder.

I thought of climbing the web to that monstrous body, and trying to make a great rent in the purple sac, so that I should fall more swiftly. But I could only have succeeded in entangling myself more thoroughly in the adhesive coils. And I dismissed the scheme when I realized that if I fell too rapidly, I might be killed upon striking the surface.

Alter the first few minutes of the flight, I could see that the balloon was sinking slowly, as the gas escaped through the bullet holes in the muscular sac. I could only wait, and fix in my mind the route that I must follow back to the machine.

The wind bore me so swiftly along that within an hour the triple peak that I watched had dropped below the curved horizon. But still I was above the great valley, so that I should be able to find my way back by following the river. I wondered if I could build a raft, and float down it, with the current.

The balloon was carried along less rapidly as it approached the surface. But, as I neared the jungle, it was evident that it still drifted at considerable speed.

Hanging helpless in the end of the red web, I anxiously scanned the jungle into which I was descending. Like that which I had first seen, it was of dense tangles of the thorny yellow scrub, broken with areas covered largely with the luxuriant green creeper.

I knew I would never be able to extricate myself alive if I had the misfortune to fall in the thorn-brush. And another danger occurred to me. Even if I first touched ground in an open space, the balloon, if the wind continued to blow, would drag me into the spiky scrub before I could tear myself free of the web.

Could I cut myself free, within a safe distance of the ground, and let the balloon go on without me? It seemed that only thus could I escape being dragged to death. I knew that I could survive a fall from a considerable height, since the moon's acceleration of gravity is only about two feet per second. If only I could land on open ground!

But how could I cut the web? I was without a knife. I thought madly of attempting to bite it in two, realized that that would be as hopeless as attempting to bite through a manila rope.

But I still had the pistol. If I should place the muzzle against the cable and fire, the bullet should cut it.

I reached into my pocket again, past the adhesive coil, and found two cartridges. Though they clung to my sticky fingers, I got them at last into the magazine, and worked the action to throw one into the chamber.

By the time I had finished loading, I was low over an apparently endless jungle of the yellow thorns. Swaying on the end of the web, I was swept along over the spiky scrub, dropping swiftly. At last I could see the edge, and a green patch of the great creepers. For a time I hoped that I would be carried clear of the thorns.

Then they seemed suddenly to leap at me. I threw up my arms, to shelter my face, still clinging fiercely to the pistol.

In an instant, I was being dragged through the cruel yellow spikes. There was a sharp, dry, crackling sound, as they broke beneath my weight. A thousand sharp, poisoned bayonets scratched at me, stabbed, cut.

INTOLERABLE agony racked me. I screamed. The razor-sharp spikes were tipped with poison, so that the slightest scratch burned like liquid flame. And many of the stabbing points went deep.

It seems that I struck near the edge of the thicket. For a moment I hung there in the thorns. Then, as a harder puff of wind struck it, the balloon leaped into the air, dragging me free. I swung up like a pendulum. And down again, beyond the thorny scrub—over a strip of bare sand beside the thicket.

Bleeding rapidly from my cuts, and suffering unendurable pain from the poison in my wounds, I realized that I could not long remain conscious.

Moving in a haze of agony, I seized the red cable with one hand, put the muzzle of the automatic against it, then pulled the trigger. The report was crashing, stunning. My right hand, holding the gun, was flung back by the recoil—I should have lost the weapon had it not been glued to my fingers. The cable was jerked with terrific force, almost breaking my left hand, with which I held it.

And it parted! I plunged downward, hit with a thump, and sprawled on the sand.

For a few minutes I remained conscious as I lay there on the hard, cold sand; the first soil—I recall thinking vaguely in my agony—that I had seen not covered with vegetation.

The clothing had been half stripped from my tortured body by the thorns. I was bleeding freely from several deeper cuts—I remember how dark the blood was, sinking into the white sand.

All my body throbbed with insufferable pain, from the poison in my wounds. As if I had been plunged into a sea of flame. Only my face had been spared.

Weakly, dizzy with pain, I tried to stagger to my feet. But a coil of the red web still clung about my legs. It tripped me, and I fell forward again, upon the white sand.

I fell into bitter despair. Into blind, hopeless rage at my inane lack of caution in leaving the machine. At my foolhardiness in venturing into the edge of the jungle. Fell into gentle oblivion...

A curious sound drew me back into wakefulness. A thin, high-pitched piping, pleasantly melodious. The musical notes beat insistently upon my brain, evidently originating quite near me...

On first awakening, I was aware of no bodily sensation. My mind was peculiarly dull and slow. I was unable to recall where I was. My first impression was that I was lying in bed in my old rooming place at Midland and that my alarm clock was ringing. But soon I realized that the liquid piping notes that had disturbed me came from no alarm.

I forced open heavy eyes. What startling nightmare was this? A tangle of green creepers, incredibly profuse. A wall of yellow thorns. A scarlet mountain beyond. And purple balloons floating in a rich blue sky.

I tried to sit up. My body burst into screaming agony when I moved. And I sank back. My skin was stiff with dry blood. The deeper wounds were aching. And the poison from the thorns seemed to have stiffened my muscles, so that the slightest motion brought exquisite pain.

The melodious pipings had been abruptly silenced at my movement. But now they rose again. Behind me. I tried to turn my head.

Recollection was returning swiftly. My uncle's telegram. The flight through space and time. My expedition to the jungle's edge, and its horrible sequel. I still lay where I had fallen, on the bare sand below the spiky scrub.

I groaned despite myself, with the pain of my stiff body. The thin musical notes stopped again. And the thing that had voiced them glided around before me, so that I could see it.

A strange and wonderful being.

Its body was slender, flexible as an eel. Perhaps five feet long, it was little thicker than my upper arm. Soft, short golden down or fur covered it. Part of it was coiled on the sand; its head was lifted two or three feet.

A small head, not much larger than my fist. A tiny mouth, with curved lips full and red as a woman's. And large eyes, dark and intelligent. They were deeply violet, almost luminous. Somehow they looked human, perhaps only because they mirrored the human qualities of curiosity and pity.

Aside from red mouth and dark eyes, the head had no human features. Golden down covered it. On the crown was a plume or crest of brilliant blue. But strange as it was, it possessed a certain beauty. A beauty of exquisite proportion, of smooth curves.

Curious wing-like appendages or mantles grew from the sides of the sleek, golden body, just below the head.

Now they were stiffened, extended as if for flight. They were very white, of thin soft membrane. Their snowy surfaces were finely veined with scarlet.

Other than these white, membranous mantles, the creature had no limbs. It had a slim, long, pliant body, covered with golden fur; a small, delicate head with red mouth; warm dark eyes, crested with blue, and delicate wings thrust out from its sides.

I stared at it.

Even at first sight, I did not fear it, though I was helpless. It seemed to have a magnetic power that filled me with quiet confidence, assured me that it meant only good.

The lips pursed themselves. And the thin, musical piping sound came from them again. Was the thing speaking to me? I uttered the first phrases that entered my mind, "Hello. Who are we, anyhow?"

CHAPTER FIVE
The Mother

THE thing glided toward me swiftly, its smooth round golden body leaving a little twisting track in the white sand. It lowered its head a little. And it laid one of the white mantles across my forehead.

The strange red-veined membrane was soft, yet there was an odd firmness in its pressure against my skin. A vital warmth seemed to come from it—it was vibrant with energy, with life.

The pipings came again. And they seemed to stir vague response in my mind, to call dim thoughts into being. As the same sounds were repeated again and again, definite questions formed in my mind.

"What are you? How did you come here?"

Through some strange telepathy induced by the pressure of the mantle upon my head, I was grasping the thought in the piping words.

It was a little time before I was sufficiently recovered from my astonishment to speak. Then I replied slowly, phrasing my expressions carefully, and uttering them as distinctly as I could.

"I am a native of Earth, of the great white globe you can see in the sky. I came here on a machine that moves through space and time. I left it, and was caught and jerked up into the air by one of those purple, floating things. I broke the web, and fell here. My body was so torn by the thorns that I cannot move."

The thing piped again. A single quavering note. It was repeated until its meaning formed in my mind.

"I understand."

"Who are you?" I ventured.

I got the meaning of the reply, as it was being piped for the third time. "I am the Mother. The Eternal Ones, who destroyed my people, pursue me. To escape them, I am going to the sea."

And the thin, musical tones came again. This time I understood them more easily.

"Your body seems slow to heal its hurts. Your mental force is feeble. May I aid you?"

"Of course," I said. "Anything you can do—"

"Lie still. Trust me. Do not resist. You must sleep," When the meaning of the notes came to me, I relaxed upon the sand and closed my eyes.

I could feel the warm, vibrant pressure of the mantle on my forehead. Vital, throbbing force seemed pulsing into me through it. I felt no fear, despite the strangeness of my situation. A living wave of confidence came over me. Serene trust in the power of this being. I felt a command to sleep. I did not resist it; a strong tide of vital energy swept me into oblivion.

It seemed but an instant later, though it must have been many hours, when an insistent voice called me back from sleep.

Vitality filled me. Even before I opened my eyes, I was conscious of a new and abounding physical vigor, of perfect health; I was bubbling with energy and high spirits. And I knew, by the complete absence of bodily pain, that my wounds were completely healed.

I opened my lids, saw the amazing creature that had called itself the Mother. Its smooth golden body coiled beside me on the sand. Its large, clear eyes watching me intently, with kind sympathy.

Abruptly I sat up. My limbs were stiff no longer. My body was still caked with dried blood, clothed in my tattered garments; the sticky scarlet coils of the web were still around me. But my ragged wounds were closed. Only white scars showed where they had been.

"Why, I'm well!" I told the Mother, thankfully. "How'd you do it?"

The strange being piped melodiously, and I grasped the meaning almost at once. "My vital force is stronger than your own. I merely lent you energy."

I began tearing at the coils of the crimson web about me. Their viscid covering seemed to have dried a little; otherwise I might never have got them off. After a moment the Mother glided forward and helped.

It used the white, membranous appendages like hands. Though they appeared quite frail, they seemed able to grasp the red cable powerfully when they were folded about it.

In a few minutes I was on my feet.

Again the Mother piped at me. I failed to understand, though vague images were summoned to my mind. I knelt down again on the sand, and the being glided toward me, pressed the white, red-veined mantle once more against my forehead. An amazing organ, that mantle, so delicately beautiful. So strong of grasp when used as a hand. And useful, as I was to learn, as an organ of some strange sense.

The meaning of the pipings came to me clearly now, with the warm, vibrant mantle touching my head.

"Adventurer, tell me more of your world, and how you came here. My people are old, and I have vital powers beyond your own. But we have never been able to go beyond the atmosphere of our planet. Even the Eternal Ones, with all their machines, have never been able to bridge the gulf of space. And it has been thought that the primary planet from which you say you came is yet too hot for the development of life."

FOR many hours we talked, I in my natural voice, the Mother in those weirdly melodious pipings. At first the transference of thought by the telepathy which the wonderful mantle made possible was slow and awkward. I, especially, had trouble in receiving, and had many times to ask the Mother to repeat a complex thought. But facility increased with practice, and I at last was able to understand, quite readily, even when the white membrane did not touch me.

The sun had been low when I woke. It set, and the dew fell upon us. We talked on in the darkness. And the Earth rose, illuminating the jungle with argent glory. Still we talked, until it was day again. For a time the air was quite cold. Wet with the abundant dew, I felt chilled, and shivered.

But the Mother touched me again with the white membrane. Quick, throbbing warmth seemed to flow from it into my body, and I felt cold no longer.

I told much of the world that I had left, and of my own insignificant life upon it. Told of the machine. Of the voyage across space, and back through eons of time, to this young moon.

And the Mother told me of her life, and of her lost people.

She had been the leader of a community of beings that had lived on the highlands, near the source of the great river that I had seen. A community in some respects resembling those of ants or bees upon the Earth. It had contained thousands of neuter beings, imperfectly developed females, workers. And herself, the only member capable of reproduction. She was now the sole survivor of that community.

It seemed that her race was very old, and had developed a high civilization. The Mother admitted that her people had had no machines or buildings of any kind. She declared that such things were marks of barbarism, and that her own culture was superior to mine.

"Once we had machines," she told me. "My ancient mothers lived in shells of metal and wood, such as you describe. And constructed machines to aid and protect their weak and inefficient bodies.

"But the machines tended to weaken their poor bodies still further. Their limbs atrophied, perished from lack of use. Even their brains were injured, for they lived an easy life, depending upon machines for existence facing no new problems.

"Some of my people awoke to the danger. They left the cities, and returned to the forest and the sea, to live sternly, to depend upon their own minds and their own bodies, to remain living things, and not grow into cold machines.

"The mothers divided. And my people were those that returned to the forest."

"And what," I asked, "of those that remained in the city, that kept the machines?"

"They became the Eternal Ones—my enemies.

"Generation upon generation their bodies wasted away. Until they were no longer natural animals. They became mere brains, with eyes and feeble tentacles. In place of bodies, they use machines. Living brains, with bodies of metal.

"Too weak, they became, to reproduce their kind. So they sought immortality, with their mechanical science. And still some of them live on, in their ugly city of metal—though for ages no young have been born among them. The Eternal Ones.

"But at last they die, because that is the way of life. Even with all their knowledge they cannot live forever. One by one, they fall. Their strange machines are still, with rotting brains in their cases.

"And the few thousands that live attacked my people. They planned to take the Mothers. To change their offspring with their hideous arts, and make of them new brains for the machines.

"The Mothers were many, when the war began. And my people a thousand times more. Now only I remain. But it was no easy victory for the Eternal Ones. My people fought bravely. Many an ancient brain they killed. But the Eternal Ones had great engines of war that we could not escape, nor destroy with our vital energy.

"All the Mothers save myself were taken. And all destroyed themselves rather than have their children made into living machines.

"I alone escaped. Because my people sacrificed their lives for me. In my body are the seed of a new race. I seek a home for my children. I have left our old land on the shores of the lake, and I am going down to the sea. There we shall be far from the Eternal Land. And perhaps our enemies will never find us.

"But the Eternal Ones know I have escaped. They are hunting me. Hunting me with their strange machines."

When day came, I felt very hungry. What was I to do for food in this weird jungle? Even if I could find fruits or nuts, how could I tell whether they were poisonous? I mentioned my hunger.

"Come," the Mother piped.

She glided away across the white sand, with easy, sinuous grace. Very beautiful, she was. Slim body, smooth, rounded. Compactly trim. The golden down was bright in the sunlight; sapphire rays played over the blue plume upon her head. The wondrous, red-veined mantles at her sides shone brilliantly.

Regarding her strange beauty, I stood still for a moment, and then moved after her slowly, absently.

She turned back suddenly, with something like humor flashing in her great dark violet eyes.

"Is your great body so slow you cannot keep up with me?" she piped, almost derisively. "Shall I carry you?" Her eyes were mocking.

FOR answer I crouched, then leaped into the air. My wild spring carried me a score of feet above her, and beyond. I had the misfortune to come down headfirst upon the sand, though I received no injury.

I saw laughter in her eyes, as she glided swiftly to me, and grasped my arm with one of the white mantles to assist me to my feet.

"You could travel splendidly if there were two of you, one to help the other out of the thorns," she said quaintly.

A little embarrassed by her mockery, I followed meekly.

We reached a mass of the green creeper. Without hesitation, she pushed on through the feathery foliage. I broke through behind her. She led the way to one of the huge white flowers, bent it toward her, and crept into it like a golden bee.

In a moment she emerged with mantles cupped up to hold a good quantity of white, crystalline powder which she had scraped from the inside of the huge calyx.

She made me hold my hands, and dropped part of the powder into them. She lifted what she had left, upon the other mantle, and began delicately licking at it with her lips.

I tasted it. It was sweet, with a peculiar, though not at all unpleasant flavor. It formed a sort of gum as it was wetted in my mouth, and this softened and dissolved as I continued to chew. I took a larger bite, and soon finished all the Mother had given me, we visited another bloom. This time I reached in and scraped out the powder with my own hand. (The crystals must have been formed for the same purpose as the nectar in terrene flowers—to attract raiders, which carry the pollen.)

I divided my booty with the Mother. She accepted but little, and I found enough of the sweetish powder in the calyx to satisfy my own hunger.

"Now I must go on down to the sea," she piped. "Too long already have I delayed with you. For I carry the seed of my race; I must not neglect the great work that has fallen upon me.

"But I was glad to know of your strange planet. And it is good to be with an intelligent being again, when I had been so long alone. I wish I could stay longer with you. But my wishes are not my master."

Thoughts of parting from her were oddly disturbing. My feeling for her was partly gratitude for saving my life and partly something else, a sense of comradeship. We were companion adventurers in this weird and lonely jungle. Solitude and my human desire for society of any sort drew me toward her.

Then came an idea. She was going down the valley to the sea. And my way led in the same direction, until I could see the triple peak that marked the location of the machine.

"May I travel with you," I asked her, "until we reach the mountain where I left the machine in which I came to your world?"

The Mother looked at me with fine dark eyes. And glided suddenly nearer. A white membranous mantle folded about my hand, with warm pressure.

"I am glad you wish to go with me," she piped. "But you must think of the danger. Remember that I am hunted by the Eternal Ones. They will doubtless destroy you if they find us together."

"I have a weapon," I said. "I'll put up a scrap for you, if we get in a tight place. And besides, I'd very likely be killed, in one way or another, if I tried to travel alone."

"Let us go, Adventurer."

Thus it was decided.

I had dropped the camera, the binoculars, and the vacuum bottle when the balloon creature jerked me into the air. They were lost in the jungle. But I still had the automatic. It had remained in my hand—stuck to it, in fact—when I fell upon the sand. I carried it with me.

The Mother objected to the weapon. Because it was a machine, and machines weakened all that used them. But I insisted that we should have to fight machines, if the Eternal Ones caught us, and that fire could be best fought with fire. She yielded gracefully.

"But my vital force will prove stronger than your rude slaying machine. Adventurer," she maintained.

We set out almost immediately. She glided oft along the strip of bare sand beside the wall of thorny yellow scrub. And began my instruction in the ways of life upon the moon, by informing me that there was always such a clear zone about a thicket of the thorn-brush, because its roots generated a poison in the soil which prevented the growth of other vegetation near them.

When we had traveled two or three miles, we came to a crystal pool, where the abundant dew had collected at the bottom of a bare, rocky slope. We drank there. Then the Mother plunged into it joyously. With white mantles folded tight against her sides, she flashed through the water like a golden eel. I was glad to remove my own garments, and wash the grime and dried blood from my body.

I was donning my tattered clothing again, and the Mother was lying beside me, at the edge of the pool, with eyes closed, drying her golden fur in the sunshine, when I saw the ghostly bars.

Seven thin upright pillars of light, ringed about us. Straight bars of pale white radiance. They stood like phantom columns about us, inclosing a space ten yards across. They were not above two inches in diameter. And they were quite transparent, so I could see the green jungle and the yellow wall of thorn-brush quite plainly through them.

I was not particularly alarmed. In fact, I thought the ghostly pillars only some trick of my vision. I rubbed my eyes, and said rather carelessly to the Mother:

"Are the spirits building a fence around us? Or is it just my eyes?"

She lifted her golden, blue-crested head quickly. Her violet eyes went suddenly wide. I saw great alarm in them. Terror. And she moved with astonishing speed. She drew her slender length into a coil. Leaped. And seized my shoulder as she leaped, with one of her mantles.

She jerked me between two of those strange columns of motionless light and out of the area they enclosed.

I fell on the sand, got quickly to my feet.

"What—" I began.

"The Eternal Ones," her sweet, whistling tones came swiftly. "They have found me. Even here, they reach me with their evil power. We must go on, quickly."

She glided swiftly away. Still buttoning my clothing, I followed, keeping pace with her easily, with my regular leaps of half a dozen yards. Followed, wondering vainly what danger there might have been in the pillars of ghostly light.

CHAPTER SIX
Pursuit!

WE SKIRTED a continuous wall of the spiky yellow scrub.

The strip of clear ground we followed was usually fifty to one hundred yards wide. The mass of yellow thorn-brush, the poison from whose roots had killed the vegetation here, rose dense and impenetrable to our right. To the left of our open way were limitless stretches covered with the green creeper. Undulating seas of feathery emerald foliage. Scattered with huge white blooms. Broken, here and there, with strange plants of various kinds. Beyond were other clumps of the yellow scrub. A red mountain wall rose in the distance. Huge purple balloons swayed here and there upon this weird, sunlit moonscape, anchored with their red cables.

I suppose we followed that open strip for ten miles. I was beginning to breathe heavily, which was caused by the combination of the hard exercise of walking and the moon's light atmosphere. The Mother showed no fatigue.

Abruptly she paused ahead of me, then glided into a sort of tunnel through the forest of thorns. A passage five feet wide and six feet high, with the yellow spokes arching over it. The floor was worn smooth, hard-packed as if by constant use. It seemed almost perfectly straight, for I could see down it for a considerable distance. Twilight filled it, filtering down through the unbroken mass of cruel bayonets above.

"I am not eager to use this path," the Mother told me. "For they who made it are hostile things. And though not very intelligent, they are able to resist my vital force, so that I cannot control them. We shall be helpless if they discover us.

"But there is no other way. We must cross this forest of thorns. And I am glad to be out of sight in this tunnel. Perhaps the Eternal Ones will lose us again. We must hasten, and hope that we encounter no rightful user of the path. If one appears, we must hide."

I was placed immediately at a disadvantage upon entering the tunnel, for I could no longer take the long leaps by which I had been traveling. My pace became a sort of trot. I had to hold my head down to save it from the poisoned thorns above.

The Mother glided easily before me, to my relief not in such haste as before. Slender and strong and trimly beautiful—for all her strangeness. I was glad she had let me come with her. Even if peril threatened.

I found breath for speech.

Those ghostly bars," I panted. "What were they?" ·

"The Eternal Ones possess strange powers of science," came the thin, whistling notes of her reply. "Something like the television you told me of. But more highly developed. They were able to see us back by the pool.

"And the shining bars were projected through space by their rays of force. They meant some harm to us.

Just what, I do not know. It is apparently a new weapon, which they did not use in the war."

We must have gone many miles through the tunnel. It had been almost perfectly straight. There had been no branches or cross passages. We had come through no open space. Roof and walls of yellow thorns had been unbroken. I was wondering what sort of creature it might be that had made a path through the thorns so long and straight.

The Mother stopped suddenly and turned back to face me.

"One of the makers of the trail is approaching," she piped. "I feel it coming. Wait for me a bit."

She sank in golden coils upon the trail. Her head was raised a little. The mantles were extended stiffly. Always before they had been white, except for their fine veining of red. But now soft, rosy colors flushed them. Her full red lips were parted a little, and her eyes had become strange, wide, staring. They seemed to look past me, to gaze upon scenes far off, invisible to ordinary sight.

For long seconds she remained motionless, violet eyes distant, staring.

Then she stirred abruptly and rose upon tawny, golden coils. Alarm was in her great eyes, in her thin, melodious tones.

"The creature comes behind us. Upon this trail. We have scant time to reach the open, we must go swiftly."

She waited for me to begin my stumbling run, glided easily beside me. I moved awkwardly. With only the moon's slight gravitational pull to hold me to the trail, I was in constant danger from the thorns.

For tortured hours, it seemed to me, we raced down the straight passage, through the unbroken forest of yellow thorns. My heart was laboring painfully; my breath came in short gasps of agony. My body was not equipped for such prolonged exertions in the light air.

The Mother, just ahead of me, glided along with effortless ease. I knew that she could easily have left me, had she wished.

At last I stumbled, fell headlong, and did not have energy to get at once to my feet. My lungs burned, my heart was a great ache. Sweat was pouring from me; my temples throbbed; and a red mist obscured my sight.

"Go—on," I gasped, between panting breaths. "I'll try—to stop—it."

I fumbled weakly for my gun.

The Mother stopped, then came back to me. Her piping notes were quick, insistent. "Come. We are near the open now. And the thing is close. You must come!"

With a soft, flexible mantle she seized my arm. It seemed to me that a wave of new strength and energy came into me from it. At any rate, I staggered to my feet, lurched forward again. As I rose, I cast a glance backward.

A dark, indistinguishable shape was in view. So large that it filled almost the whole width of the tunnel. A dim circle of the pale light of the thorn forest showed around it.

I ran on...on...on.

MY LEGS rose and fell, rose and fell, like the insensate levers of an automaton. I felt no sensation from them. Even my lungs had ceased to burn since the

Mother touched me. And my heart ached no longer. It seemed that I floated beside my body, and watched it run, run, run with the monotonously repeated movements of a machine.

My eyes were upon the Mother before me.

Gliding so swiftly through the twilight of the tunnel. Trim, round golden body. White mantles extended stiffly, wing-like, as if to help carry her. Delicate head raised, the blue plume upon it flashing.

I watched that blue plume as I ran. It danced mockingly before me, always retreating. Always just beyond my grasp. I followed it through the blinding mists of fatigue, when all the rest of the world melted into a ray blue, streaked with bloody crimson.

I was astonished when we came out into the sunlight. A strip of sand below the yellow wall of thorns. Cool green foliage beyond, a sea of green. Sinister purple balloons above it, straining on crimson cables. Far off, a scarlet line of mountains, steep and rugged.

The Mother turned to the left.

I followed, automatically, mechanically. I was beyond feeling. I could see the bright moonscape, but it was strange no longer. Even the threat of the purple balloons was remote, without consequence.

I do not know how far we ran beside the forest of horns before the Mother turned again and led the way into a mass of creepers.

"Lie still," she piped. "The creature may not find us."

Gratefully, I flung myself down in the delicate fronds. I lay flat, with my eyes closed, my breath coming in great, painful, sobbing gasps. The Mother folded my hand in her soft mantle again, and immediately, it seemed, I felt relief, though I still breathed heavily.

"Your reserve of vital energy is very low," she commented.

I took the automatic from my pocket, examined it to see that it was ready for action. I had cleaned and loaded it before we started. I saw the Mother raising her blue-crested head cautiously. I got to my knees, peered back along the bare strip of sand, down which we had come.

I saw the thing advancing swiftly along the sand.

A sphere of bright crimson—nearly five feet in diameter. It rolled along, following the way we had come.

"It has found us!" the Mother piped, very softly. "And my vital power cannot reach through its armor. It will suck the fluids from our bodies."

I looked down at her. She had drawn her slender body into a golden coil. Her head rose in the center, and the mantles were outspread, pure white, veined with fine lines of scarlet, and frail as the petals of a lily. Her great dark eyes were grave and calm; there was no trace of panic in them.

I raised the automatic, determined to show no more fear than she, and to give my best to save her.

Now the scarlet globe was no more than fifty yards away. I could distinguish the individual scales of its armor, looking like plates of horn covered with ruby lacquer. No limbs or external appendages were visible then, but I saw dark ovals upon the shell, appearing at the top and seeming to drop down, as the thing rolled.

I began shooting.

At such a distance there was no possibility of missing. I knelt in the leaves of the green creeper, and emptied the magazine into the globe.

It continued to roll on toward us, without change of speed. But a deep, angry drumming sound came from within it. A reverberating roar of astonishing volume. After a few moments, I heard it repeated from several points about us. Low and distant rumblings, almost like thunder.

In desperate haste, I was filling the clip with fresh cartridges. Before I could snap it back into the gun, the creature was upon us.

Until it stopped, it had presented a sphere of unbroken surface. But suddenly six long, glistening black tentacles reached out of it, one from each of the black ovals I had seen evenly spaced about the reel shell. They were a dozen feet long, slender, covered with thin black skin corrugated with innumerable wrinkles, and glistening with tiny drops of moisture. At the base of each was a single, staring, black-lidded eye.

One of those black tentacles was thrust toward me.

It reeked with an overpowering, fetid odor. At its extremity was a sharp, hooked claw, beside a black opening. I think the creature sucked its food through those hideous, retractable tentacles.

I got the loaded clip into the gun, hastily snapped a cartridge into the chamber. Shrinking back from the writhing tentacular arm, I fired seven shots, as rapidly as I could press the trigger, into the black-lidded eye.

The deep drumming notes came from within the red shell again. The black tentacles writhed, thrashed about, and became suddenly stiff and rigid. The sound of it died to a curious rattle, and then ceased.

"Yon have killed it," the Mother whistled musically. "You use your machine well, and it is more powerful than I thought. Perhaps, after all, we may yet live."

As if in ominous answer, a reverberating roll of distant drumming came from the tangle of yellow thorns. She listened, and the white mantles were stiffened in her alarm.

"But it has called to its kind. Soon many will be here, we must hasten away."

THOUGH I was still so tired that movement was torture, I rose and followed the Mother, as she glided on along the sand.

Only a moment did I pause to examine the very interesting creature I had killed. It seemed unique, both in shape and in means of locomotion. It must have developed the spherical shell of red armor through ages of life in the spiky scrub. By drawing its limbs inside, it was able to crash through the thorns without suffering any hurt. I supposed it contrived to roll along by some rhythmic muscular contraction, inside the shell—such movement being much easier on the moon than it would be on Earth, because of the lesser gravity. Where it could not roll, it dragged or lifted itself with the long, muscular appendages that I have called tentacles.

Since we were in the open air again, I was able to resume my progression by deliberate, measured leaps, which carried me forward as fast as the Mother could move, and with much less effort than I had spent in running. I had a few moments of rest as I glided through the air between leaps, which compensated for the fiercer effort of each spring.

From time to time I looked back, nervously. At first I could see only the scarlet shell of the dead creature, there by the green vines where we had killed it. Always smaller, until it was hardly visible.

Then I saw other spheres. Emerging from the tangle of yellow thorn-brush. Rolling along the strip of bare soil, to congregate about the dead being. Finally I saw that they had started in our direction, rolling along rather faster than we could move.

"They are coming," I told the Mother. "And more of them than I can kill."

"They are implacable," came her piping reply. "When one of them sets out upon the trail of some luckless creature, it never stops until it has sucked the body fluids from it—or until it is dead."

"Anything we can do?" I questioned.

"There is a rock ahead of us, beyond that thicket. A small hill, whose sides are so steep they will not be able to climb it. If we can reach it in time, we may be able to scramble to the top.

"It will be only temporary escape, since the creatures will never leave so long as we are alive upon it. But we shall delay our fate, at least—if we can reach it in time."

Again I looked back. Our pursuers were rolling along like a group of red marbles, at the edge of the yellow forest. Gaining upon us—swiftly.

The Mother glided along more rapidly. The white mantles were stiffly extended from her golden sides, and aglow with rosy colors. The muscles beneath her furry skin rippled evenly, gracefully.

I increased the force of my own leaps.

We rounded an arm of the tangle of scrub, then came in sight of the rock. A jutting mass of black granite. Its sides leaped up steep and bare from a mass of green creepers. Green moss crowned it. Thirty feet high it was. Perhaps a hundred in length.

Our pursuers were no longer merely marbles when we saw the rock. They had grown to the size of baseballs, rolling swiftly after us.

The Mother glided on, a tireless strength in her graceful tawny body. And I leaped desperately, straining to drive myself as fast as possible.

We turned and broke through the thick masses of verdure to the rock. For a moment we then stood beneath its sheer wall, grim and black.

The red spheres were no more than a hundred yards behind. A sudden rumble of drums came from them when we halted by the rock. I could see the dark ovals on their glistening red armor, which marked their eyes and the ends of their concealed tentacles.

"I can never climb that," the Mother was piping.

"I can leap up!" I cried. "Earth muscles. I'll carry you up."

"Better that one should live than both of us die," she said. "I can delay them, until you reach the top."

She started gliding back, toward the swiftly rolling spheres.

I bent and snatched her up.

It was the first time that I had felt her body. The golden fur was short, and very soft. The rounded body beneath it was firm, muscular, warm and vibrant. It throbbed with life. I felt that a strange sudden surge of energy was coming into me from contact with it.

I threw her quickly over my shoulder, ran forward a few steps, and leaped desperately up at that sheer wall of black granite.

My own weight, on the moon, was only thirty pounds. The Mother, compact and strong though she was, weighed no more than a third as much. Combined, our weight was then some forty pounds. But, as she had realized, it was an apparently hopeless undertaking to attempt to hurl that mass to the top of the cliff before us.

At first I thought I should make it, as we soared swiftly up and up, toward the crown of red moss. Then I realized that we should strike the face of the cliff before we reached the top.

The face of the black rock was sheer. But my searching eyes caught a little projecting ledge. As we fell against the vertical cliff, my fingers caught that ledge. There was a moment of dreadful uncertainty, for the ledge was mossy, slippery.

CHAPTER SEVEN
The Eternal Ones Follow!

MY LEFT hand slipped suddenly off. But the right held. I drew myself upward. The Mother slipped from my shoulder to the top of the rock. Grasped my left hand with one of the white mantles and drew me to safety.

Trembling from the strain of it, I got to my feet upon the soft scarlet moss, and surveyed our fortress. The moss-covered surface was almost level, a score of feet wide at the middle, where we stood, and a hundred in length. On all sides the walls were steep, though not everywhere so steep as where I had leaped up.

"Thank you, Adventurer," the Mother whistled musically. "You have saved my life, and the lives of all my people to come."

"I was merely repaying a debt," I told her.

We watched the red globes. Very soon they reached the foot of the cliff. The rumble of drums floated up from the group of them. And they scattered, surrounding the butte.

Presently we discovered that they were attempting to climb up. They were not strong enough to make the leap as I had done. But they were finding fissures and ledges upon which their long tentacles could find a grasp, drawing themselves up.

We patrolled the sides of the rock regularly, and I shot those that seemed to be making the best progress. I was able to aim carefully at an eye or the base of a tentacle. And usually a single shot was enough to send the climber rolling back down to the green jungle.

The view from our stronghold was magnificent. On one side was an endless wall of yellow scrub, with crimson mountains towering above it in the distance. On the other, the green tangle of the luxuriant creepers swept down to the wide silver river. Yellow and green mottled the slope that stretched up to scarlet hills beyond.

We held out for an entire day.

The sun sank beyond the red mountains when we had been upon the butte only an hour or two. A dark night would have terminated our adventures on the spot. But fortunately the huge white disk of the Earth rose almost immediately after sunset, and gave sufficient light throughout the night to enable us to see the spheres that persisted in attempting to climb the walls of our fort.

It was late on the following afternoon that I used my last shot. I turned to the Mother with the news that I could no longer keep the red spheres from the walls, that they would soon be overwhelming us.

"It does not matter," she piped. "The Eternal Ones have found us again."

Looking nervously about, I saw the bars of ghostly light once more. Seven thin upright pillars of silvery radiance, standing in a ring about us. They had exactly the same appearance as those from which we had fled at the pool.

"I have felt them watching for some time," she said.

"Before we escaped by running away. Now that is impossible."

Calmly she coiled her tawny length. The white mantles were folded against her golden fur. Her small head sank upon her coils, blue crest erect above it. Her violet eyes were grave, calm, alert. They reflected neither fear nor despair.

The seven pillars of light about us became continually brighter.

One of the red spheres, with black tentacles extended, dragged itself upon the top of the butte, with us. The Mother saw it, but paid it no heed. It was outside the ring formed by the seven pillars. I stood still, within that ring, beside the Mother, watching—waiting.

The seven columns of light grew brighter.

Then it seemed that they were no longer merely light, but solid metal.

At the same instant, I was blinded with a flash of light, intolerably bright. A splintering crash of sound smote my ears, sharp as the crack of a rifle, infinitely louder. A wave of pain flashed over my body, as if I had received a severe electric shock. I had a sense of abrupt movement, as if the rock beneath my feet had been jarred by a moonquake.

Then we were no longer upon the rock.

I was standing upon a broad, smooth metal plate. About its edge rose seven metal rods, shining with a white light, their positions corresponding exactly to the seven ghostly pillars. The Mother was coiled on the metal plate beside me, her violet eyes still cool and quiet, revealing no surprise.

But I was dazed with astonishment.

For we were no longer in the jungle. The metal plate upon which I stood was part of a complex mechanism, of bars and coils of shining wire, and huge tubes of transparent crystal, which stood in the center of a broad open court, paved with bright, worn metal.

About this court towered many buildings. Lofty, rectangular edifices of metal and transparent crystal. They were not beautiful structures. Nor were they in good repair. The metal was covered with ugly red oxide. Many of the crystal panels were shattered.

Along the metal-paved streets, and on the wide courtyard about us, things were moving. Not human beings. Not evidently, living things at all. But grotesque things of metal. Machines. They had no common standard of form; few seemed to resemble any others. They had apparently been designed with a variety of shapes, to fill a variety of purposes. But many had a semblance to living things that was horrible mockery.

"This is the land of the Eternal Ones," the Mother piped to me softly. "These are the beings that destroyed my people, seeking new brains for their worn-out machines."

"But how did we get here?" I demanded.

"EVIDENTLY they have developed means of transmitting matter through space. A mere technical question. Resolving matter into energy, transmitting the energy without loss on a light beam, condensing it again into the original atoms.

"It is not remarkable that the Eternal Ones cal do such things. When they gave up all that is life, for such power. When they sacrificed their bodies for machines. Should they not have some reward?"

"It seems impossible—"

"It must, to you. The science of your world is young. If you have television after a few hundred years, what will you not have developed after a hundred thousand?

"Even to the Eternal Ones, it is new. It is only in the time of my own life that they have been able to transmit objects between two stations, without destroying their identity. And they have never before used this apparatus, with carrier rays that could reach out to disintegrate our bodies upon the rock, and create a reflecting zone of interference that would focus the beam here—"

Her piping notes broke off sharply. Three grotesque machines were advancing upon us, about the platform. Queer bright cases, with levels and wheels projecting from them. Jointed metal limbs. Upon the top of each was a transparent crystal dome, containing a strange, shapeless gray mass. A soft helpless gray thing, with huge black staring eyes. The brain in the machine! The Eternal One.

Horrible travesties of life, were those metal things. At first they appeared almost alive, with their quick, sure movements. But mechanical sounds came from them, little clatterings and hummings. They were stark and ugly.

And their eyes roughened my skin with dread. Huge, black, and cold. There was nothing warm in them, nothing human, nothing kind. They were as emotionless as polished lenses. And filled with menace.

"They shall not take me alive!" the Mother piped, lifting herself beside me on tawny coils.

Then, as if something had snapped like a taut wire in my mind, I ran at the nearest of the Eternal Ones, my eyes searching swiftly for a weapon.

It was one of the upright metal rods that I seized. Its lower end was set in an oddly shaped mass of white crystal, which I took to be an insulator of some kind. It shattered when I threw my weight on the rod. And the rod came free in my hands, the white glow vanishing from it. I saw it was copper.

Thus I was provided with a massive metal club, as heavy as I could readily swing. On Earth, it would have weighed far more than I could lift.

Raising it over my head, I sprang in front of the foremost of the advancing machines—a case of bright metal, moving stiffly upon metal limbs, with a dome-shaped shell of crystal upon it, which housed the helpless gray brain, with its black, unpleasant eyes. I saw little tentacles—feeble translucent fingers—reaching from the brain to touch controlling levers.

The machine paused before me. An angry, insistent buzzing came from it. A great, hooked, many-jointed metal lever reached out from it suddenly, as if to seize me.

And I struck, bringing the copper bar down upon the transparent dome with all my strength. The crystal was tough, but the inertia of the copper bar was as great as it would have been upon the Earth; its hundreds of pounds came down with a force indeed terrific.

The dome was shattered. And the gray brain smashed into red pulp.

The Eternal Ones would certainly have been able to seize the Mother without suffering any harm, and probably any other creature of the moon that might have been brought with her on the matter-transmitting beam. But they were not equipped for dealing with a being whose muscles were the stronger ones of Earth.

The two companions of the Eternal One I had destroyed fell upon me. Though the copper bar was not very heavy, it was oddly hard to swing because of its great inertia. The metal limbs of the third machine closed about my body, even as I crushed the brain in the second with another smashing blow.

I squirmed desperately, but I was unable to twist about to get in a position to strike.

Then the Mother was gliding toward me. Blue crest erect upon her golden head, eager light of battle flashing in her violet eyes. From her smooth, tawny sides the mantles were stiffly outstretched. And they were almost scarlet with the flashing lights that played through them. My momentary despair vanished; I felt that she was invincible.

She almost reached me. And then rose upon her glossy coils, and gazed at the brain in the transparent dome of the machine that held me, her membranes still alight.

Abruptly the machine released me; its metal limbs were relaxed, motionless.

My encrimsoned copper mace rose and descended once more, and the machine fell with a clatter upon its side.

"My mental energy is greater than that of the Eternal One," the Mother piped in calm explanation. "I was able to interfere with its neural processes to cause paralysis." She looked about us suddenly.

"But smash the delicate parts of this machine that brought us here. So that if we have the good fortune to escape, they cannot soon bring us back. I know it is the only one they have, and it does not look as if it could be quickly repaired."

MY CLUB was busy again. Delicate coils were battered beneath it. Complex prisms and mirrors and lenses shattered. Delicate wires and grids in crystal shells, which must have been electron tubes, destroyed.

The three machines we had wrecked had been the only ones near. But a score or more of others were soon approaching across the metal-paved court, producing buzzing sounds as if of anger and excitement. Some of them were near before my work was done.

Too many of them to battle. We must attempt an escape.

I stooped, picked up the Mother's warm, downy body, and ran across the platform, toward the ring of approaching machine beings. Near them, I leaped, as high and as far as I could.

The spring carried me over them, and a good many yards beyond. In a moment I was in the middle of a worn pavement of metal. The street, almost empty of the machines, ran between ancient and ugly buildings, toward a lofty wall of some material black and brilliant as obsidian.

I hastened desperately toward the wall, moving with great leaps. The Eternal Ones followed in humming, clattering confusion, falling swiftly behind.

They had been taken quite by surprise, of course. And, as the Mother had said, dependence upon the machine had not developed in them the ability to respond quickly to emergencies.

As we later discovered, some of the machines could travel much faster than could we. But, as I have remarked, the things were not of a standard design, all differing. And none of those behind us happened to be of the fastest type.

I do not doubt that they could easily have destroyed us, as we fled. But their objective would have been defeated. They wanted the Mother alive.

We reached the shining black wall well ahead of our pursuers. Its surface was smooth and perpendicular; it was fully as high as the cliff up which I had leaped with the Mother. And there was no projecting ledge to save us if I fell short.

I paused, dropping the heavy mace.

"You could toss me up," the Mother suggested. "Then leap."

There was no time for delay. She coiled quickly up into a golden sphere. I hurled her upward, like a football. She vanished over the top of the wall. I lifted the mace, threw it up, and to one side, so it would not strike her.

The Eternal Ones were close behind—a mob-like group of grotesque machines, buzzing angrily. One of them flung some missile. There was a crashing explosion against the black wall, a flare of green light. I realized the danger of being separated from the Mother, even as I leaped.

My spring carried me completely over the wall, which was only some five or six feet thick.

I descended into a luxuriant tangle of the green creepers. Foot-thick stems covered the ground in an unbroken network, feathery leaves rising from them higher than my head. I fell on my side in the delicate foliage, then struggled quickly to my feet. The green fronds cut off my view in all directions, though I could see the top of the black wall above.

Before I struck the ground I had glimpsed a vast green plain lying away eastward to the horizon. In the north was a distant line of red mountains. The city of the Eternal Ones lay westward.

I saw nothing of the Mother; I could not, in truth, see a dozen feet through the exotic jungle.

"This way," her cautious whistling tones reached me in a moment. "Here is your weapon."

I broke through the masses of delicate fronds in the direction of the sound, found the Mother unharmed, coiled in a golden circle beside the copper bar. She glided silently away; I picked up the bar and followed as rapidly and quietly as I could.

Once I looked back when we passed a narrow open space and saw a little group of the Eternal Ones standing upon the black wall. They must have been looking after us, but I do not suppose they saw us.

For the rest of the day—it was early afternoon when we escaped—and all night when the jungle was weird and silvery in the Earthlight, and until late on the following day, we hastened on. We did not stop except to drink and bathe at a little stream, and to scrape the sweet white powder from a few of the great argent flowers we passed. We ate as we moved. The jungle of creepers was unbroken; we were well hidden in this luxuriant delicate foliage.

At first I had been sure we would be followed. But as the hours passed and there was no sign of pursuit, my spirits rose. I doubted now that the Eternal Ones could follow the trail swiftly enough to overtake us. But I still carried the copper mace.

The Mother was less optimistic than I was.

"I know they are following," she told me. "I feel them. But we may lose them. If they cannot repair the machine that you wrecked—and I am sure they cannot do it soon."

We had approached a rocky slope when the Mother found a little cave beneath an overhanging ledge. It was in this that we rested. Totally exhausted, I threw myself down and slept like a dead man.

It was early on the next morning when the Mother woke me. She lay coiled at the entrance of the cave, the frail mantles stiffened and flushed a little with rosy light, violet eyes grave and watchful.

"The Eternal Ones follow," she piped. "They are yet far off. But we must go on."

CHAPTER EIGHT
An Earth Man Fights

CLIMBING to the top of the rocky slope, we came out upon a vast plateau, covered with green moss. The level surface was broken here and there by low hills; but no other vegetation was in view before us. At a distance, the plain resembled a weird desert covered with green snow.

It took six days to cross the moss-grown tableland. We finished the white powder we had carried with us on the fourth day; and we found no water on the fifth or sixth. Though those days were of only eighteen hours each, we were still in a sorry plight when we descended into a valley green with the creepers. We watered ourselves in a crystal stream whose water seemed the sweetest I had ever tasted.

We ate and rested for two nights and a day, before we went on—though the Mother insisted that the Eternal Ones still followed.

Then, for seventeen days, we followed down the stream, which was joined by countless tributaries until it became a majestic river. On the seventeenth day, the river flowed into a still greater one, which came down a valley many miles wide, covered with yellow thorn brush and green creepers, and infested with thousands of the purple balloon creatures, which I had learned to avoid by keeping to the green jungle, where they could not throw their webs with accuracy.

We swam the river, and continued down the eastern bank—it was flowing generally south. Five days later we came in view of the triple peak I well remembered.

Next morning we left the jungle and climbed up to the little moss-carpeted plateau where I had left the machine. I had feared that it somehow would be gone, or wrecked. But it lay just as I had left it on the day after I landed on the moon. Bright, polished—a window-studded wall of armor between two projecting plates of gleaming copper.

We reached the door, the Mother gliding beside me.

Trembling with a great eagerness, I turned the knob and opened it. Everything was in order, just as I had left it. The oxygen cylinders, the batteries, the food refrigerator, the central control table, with the chart lying upon it.

In a week—if the mechanism worked as I hoped it would—I should be back upon the Earth. Back on Long Island. Ready to report to my uncle, and collect the first payment of my fifty thousand a year.

Still standing on the narrow deck outside the door, I looked down at the Mother.

She was coiled at my feet. The blue plume upon her golden head seemed to droop. The white mantles were limp, dragging. Her violet eyes, staring up at me, somehow seemed wistful and sad.

Abruptly an ache sprang into my heart, and my eyes dimmed, so that the bright golden image of her swam before me. I had hardly realized what her companionship had come to mean to me in our long days together.

Strange as her body was, the Mother had come to be almost human in my thoughts. Loyal, courageous, kind—a comrade.

"You must go with me," I stammered, in a voice gone oddly husky. "I don't know whether the machine will ever get back to Earth or not. But at least it will carry us out of reach of the Eternal Ones."

For the first time, the musical pipings of the Mother seemed broken and uneven, as if with emotion.

"No. We have been together long, Adventurer. And parting is not easy. But I have a great work. The seed of my kind is in me, and it must not die. The Eternal Ones are near. But I will not give up the battle until I am dead."

Abruptly she lifted her tawny length beside me. The limp, pallid mantles were suddenly bright and strong again. They seized my hands in a grasp convulsively tight. The Mother gazed up at my face, for a little time, with deep violet eyes—earnest and lonely and wistful, with the tragedy of her race in them.

Then she dropped, and glided swiftly away.

I looked after her with misty eyes, until she was half across the plateau. On her way to the sea, to find a home for the new race she was to rear. With a leaden heart, and an aching constriction in my throat, I climbed through the oval door, into the machine, and fastened it.

But I did not approach the control table. I stood at the little round windows, watching the Mother gliding away, across the carpet of moss. Going ahead alone…the last of her race…

Then I looked in the other direction, and saw the Eternal Ones. She had said the machines were near. I saw five of them. They were moving swiftly across the plateau, the way we had come.

Five grotesque machines. Their bright metal cases were larger than those of the ones we had encountered in the city. And their limbs were longer. They stalked like moving towers of metal, each upon four jointed stilts. And long, flail-like limbs dangled from the case of each. Crystal domes crowned them, sparkling in the sunlight—covering the feeble gray brains that controlled them. The Eternal Ones.

Almost at the edge of the plateau they were when I first saw them. I had time easily to finish sealing the door, to close the valve through which I had let out the excess air upon landing, and to drive up through the moon's atmosphere, toward the white planet.

But I did not move to do those things. I stood at the window watching, hands clenched so that nails cut into my palms, set teeth biting through my lip.

THEN, as they came on, I moved suddenly, governed not by reason but by an impulse that I could not resist. I opened the door and clambered hastily out, picking up the great copper mace that I had left lying outside.

And I crouched beside the machine, waiting.

Looking across the way the Mother had gone, I saw her at the edge of the plateau. A tiny, distant form, upon the green moss. I think she had already seen the machines, and realizing the futility of flight had turned back to face them.

As the machine things came by, I was appalled at their size. The metal stilts were fully six feet long, the vulnerable crystal domes eight feet above the ground.

I leaped up, and struck at the brain of the nearest as it passed. My blow crushed the transparent shell and the soft brain within it. But the machine toppled toward me, and I fell with it to the ground, cruelly bruised beneath its angular levers.

One leg was fast beneath it, pinned against the ground, and its weight was so great that I could not immediately extricate myself. But I had clung to the copper bar, and when another machine bent down, as if to examine the fallen one, I seized the weapon with both hands, and placed another fatal blow.

The second machine fell stiffly beside me, an odd humming sound continuing within it, in such a position that it almost concealed me from the others. I struggled furiously to free my leg, while the other Eternal Ones gathered about, producing curious buzzing sounds.

At last I was free, and on my knees. Always slow in such an unexpected emergency, the machine beings had taken no action, though they continued the buzzing.

One of them sprang toward me as I moved, striking a flailing blow at me with a metal arm. I leaped up at it, avoiding the sweeping blow, and struck its crystal case with the end of the copper bar.

The bar smashed through the crystal dome, and crushed the frail brain-thing within it. But the machine still moved. It went leaping away across the plateau, its metal limbs still going through the same motions as before I had killed the ruling brain.

I fell back to the ground, rolling over quickly to avoid its stalking limbs, and struggling to my feet, still holding grimly to the copper bar.

The remaining machine beings rushed upon me, flailing out with metal limbs. In complete desperation, I leaped into the air, rising ten feet above their glistening cases. I came down upon the case of one, beside the crystal dome that housed its brain. I braced my feet and struck, before it could snatch at me with its hooked levers.

As it fell to the moss, humming, buzzing, and threshing about with bright metal limbs, I leaped from it toward the other, holding the bar before me. But I struck only the metal case, without harming it, and fell from it into the moss.

Before I could stir, the thing drove its metal limb down upon my body. It struck my chest with a force that was agonizing…crushing. A rocket of fiery pain seemed to burst in my brain. For a moment I think I was unconscious. Then I was coughing up bloody foam.

I lay on the red moss, unable to move, the grim realization that I would die was breaking over me in a black wave, which swept away even my pain. The metal limb had been lifted from me.

Then the Mother was beside me. She had come back.

Her warm smooth furry body was pressed close against my side. I saw her violet eyes, misty, appealing. She laid the rose-flushed mantles over my side. The pain went suddenly from it. And I felt new strength, so I could rise up to my feet, though red mist still came from my nostrils, and I felt a hot stream of blood down my side.

The remaining machine monster was bending, reaching for the Mother. I seized the copper mace once again, struck a furious blow at the crystal shell that housed its brain. As it crashed down, beating about blindly and madly with its great metal limbs, my new strength went suddenly from me and I fell again, coughing once more.

A flailing limb struck the Mother a terrific blow, flinging her against the moss many yards away. She crept back to me, brokenly, slowly. Her golden fur was stained with crimson. Her mantles were limp and pale. There was agony in her eyes.

She came to where I lay, collapsed against my side. Very low, her musical tones reached my ears and died abruptly with a choking sound. She had tried to tell me something, and could not.

The last of the Eternal Ones that had followed was dead, and presently the machines ceased their humming and buzzing and threshing about upon the moss.

Through the rest of the day we lay there, side by side, both unable to move. And through the strange night, when the huge white disk of the Earth bathed us in silvery splendor, and in my delirium I dreamed alternately of my life upon it, and of my adventures upon this weird moon world, with the Mother.

When the argent Earth was low, and we were cold and drenched with dew, lying very close together to benefit from each other's warmth, the wild dream, passed. For a few minutes I was coldly sane. I looked back upon a life that had never had any great purpose, that had been lived carelessly, and impulsively. And I was not sorry that I had come to the moon.

I remained with the Mother until she stirred no more, and no effort on my part could rouse her to life. With tears in my eyes, I buried her beneath the green moss.

Then stumbling to the ship, I climbed in. Sealing the door and starting the machinery, I felt the ship lift quickly toward the distant beckoning Earth.

THE END

If you've enjoyed this book, you will not want to miss these terrific titles…

ARMCHAIR SCI-FI & HORROR DOUBLE NOVELS, $12.95 each

D-81 **THE LAST PLEA** by Robert Bloch
THE STATUS CIVILIZATION by Robert Sheckley

D-82 **WOMAN FROM ANOTHER PLANET** by Frank Belknap Long
HOMECALLING by Judith Merril

D-83 **WHEN TWO WORLDS MEET** by Robert Moore Williams
THE MAN WHO HAD NO BRAINS by Jeff Sutton

D-84 **THE SPECTRE OF SUICIDE SWAMP** by E. K. Jarvis
IT'S MAGIC, YOU DOPE! by Jack Sharkey

D-85 **THE STARSHIP FROM SIRIUS** by Rog Phillips
FINAL WEAPON by Everett Cole

D-86 **TREASURE ON THUNDER MOON** by Edmond Hamilton
TRAIL OF THE ASTROGAR by Henry Haase

D-87 **THE VENUS ENIGMA** by Joe Gibson
THE WOMAN IN SKIN 13 by Paul W. Fairman

D-88 **THE MAD ROBOT** by William P. McGivern
THE RUNNING MAN by J. Holly Hunter

D-89 **VENGEANCE OF KYVOR** by Randall Garrett
AT THE EARTH'S CORE by Edgar Rice Burroughs

D-90 **DWELLERS OF THE DEEP** by Don Wilcox
NIGHT OF THE LONG KNIVES by Fritz Leiber

ARMCHAIR SCIENCE FICTION CLASSICS, $12.95 each

C-28 **THE MAN FROM TOMORROW**
by Stanton A. Coblentz

C-29 **THE GREEN MAN OF GRAYPEC**
by Festus Pragnell

C-30 **THE SHAVER MYSTERY, Book Four**
by Richard S. Shaver

ARMCHAIR MASTERS OF SCIENCE FICTION SERIES, $16.95 each

MS-7 **MASTERS OF SCIENCE FICTION AND FANTASY, Vol. Seven**
Lester del Rey, "The Band Played On" and other tales

MS-8 **MASTERS OF SCIENCE FICTION, Vol. Eight**
Milton Lesser, "'A' as in Android" and other tales

If you've enjoyed this book, you will not want to miss these terrific titles...

ARMCHAIR SCI-FI & HORROR DOUBLE NOVELS, $12.95 each

D-91 **THE TIME TRAP** by Henry Kuttner
THE LUNAR LICHEN by Hal Clement

D-92 **SARGASSO OF LOST STARSHIPS** by Poul Anderson
THE ICE QUEEN by Don Wilcox

D-93 **THE PRINCE OF SPACE** by Jack Williamson
POWER by Harl Vincent

D-94 **PLANET OF NO RETURN** by Howard Browne
THE ANNIHILATOR COMES by Ed Earl Repp

D-95 **THE SINISTER INVASION** by Edmond Hamilton
OPERATION TERROR by Murray Leinster

D-96 **TRANSIENT** by Ward Moore
THE WORLD-MOVER by George O. Smith

D-97 **FORTY DAYS HAS SEPTEMBER** by Milton Lesser
THE DEVIL'S PLANET by David Wright O'Brien

D-98 **THE CYBERENE** by Rog Phillips
BADGE OF INFAMY by Lester del Rey

D-99 **THE JUSTICE OF MARTIN BRAND** by Raymond A. Palmer
BRING BACK MY BRAIN by Dwight V. Swain

D-100 **WIDE-OPEN PLANET** by L. Sprague de Camp
AND THEN THE TOWN TOOK OFF by Richard Wilson

ARMCHAIR SCIENCE FICTION CLASSICS, $12.95 each

C-31 **THE GOLDEN GUARDSMEN**
by S. J. Byrne

C-32 **ONE AGAINST THE MOON**
by Donald A. Wollheim

C-33 **HIDDEN CITY**
by Chester S. Geier

ARMCHAIR SCI-FI & HORROR GEMS SERIES, $12.95 each

G-9 **SCIENCE FICTION GEMS, Vol. Five**
Clifford D. Simak and others

G-10 **HORROR GEMS, Vol. Five**
E. Hoffman Price and others

If you've enjoyed this book, you will not want to miss these terrific titles...

ARMCHAIR SCI-FI & HORROR DOUBLE NOVELS, $12.95 each

D-101   **THE CONQUEST OF THE PLANETS** by John W. Campbell
       THE MAN WHO ANNEXED THE MOON by Bob Olsen

D-102   **WEAPON FROM THE STARS** by Rog Phillips
       THE EARTH WAR by Mack Reynolds

D-103   **THE ALIEN INTELLIGENCE** by Jack Williamson
       INTO THE FOURTH DIMENSION by Ray Cummings

D-104   **THE CRYSTAL PLANETOIDS** by Stanton A. Coblentz
       SURVIVORS FROM 9,000 B. C. by Robert Moore Williams

D-105   **THE TIME PROJECTOR** by David H. Keller, M.D. and David Lasser
       STRANGE COMPULSION by Philip Jose Farmer

D-106   **WHOM THE GODS WOULD SLAY** by Paul W. Fairman
       MEN IN THE WALLS by William Tenn

D-107   **LOCKED WORLDS** by Edmond Hamilton
       THE LAND THAT TIME FORGOT by Edgar Rice Burroughs

D-108   **STAY OUT OF SPACE** by Dwight V. Swain
       REBELS OF THE RED PLANET by Charles L. Fontenay

D-109   **THE METAMORPHS** by S. J. Byrne
       MICROCOSMIC BUCCANEERS by Harl Vincent

D-110   **YOU CAN'T ESCAPE FROM MARS** by E. K. Jarvis
       THE MAN WITH FIVE LIVES by David V. Reed

ARMCHAIR SCIENCE FICTION CLASSICS, $12.95 each

C-34   **30 DAY WONDER**
      by Richard Wilson

C-35   **G.O.G. 666**
      by John Taine

C-36   **RALPH 124C 41+**
      by Hugo Gernsback

ARMCHAIR SCI-FI & HORROR GEMS SERIES, $12.95 each

G-11   **SCIENCE FICTION GEMS, Vol. Six**
      Edmond Hamilton and others

G-12   **HORROR GEMS, Vol. Six**
      H. P. Lovecraft and others

If you've enjoyed this book, you will not want to miss these terrific titles…

ARMCHAIR SCI-FI & HORROR DOUBLE NOVELS, $12.95 each

D-111 **THE MOON ERA** by Jack Williamson
REVENGE OF THE ROBOTS by Howard Browne

D-112 **SON OF THE BLACK CHALICE** by Milton Lesser
SENTRY OF THE SKY by Evelyn E. Smith

D-113 **OUTPOST ON THE MOON** by Joslyn Maxwell
POTENTIAL ZERO by S. J. Byrne

D-114 **OUTPOST INFINITY** by Raymond F. Jones
THE WHITE INVADERS by Ray Cummings

D-115 **TIME TRAP** by Rog Phillips
THE COSMIC DESTROYER by Alexander Blade

D-116 **THE OTHER SIDE OF THE MOON** by Edmond Hamilton
SECRET INVASION by Walter Kubilius

D-117 **DANGER MOON** by Frederik Pohl
THE HIDDEN UNIVERSE by Ralph Milne Farley

D-118 **THE WAILING ASTEROID** by Murray Leinster
THE WORLD THAT COULDN'T BE by Clifford D. Simak

D-119 **THE WHISPERING GORILLA** by Don Wilcox
RETURN OF THE WHISPERING GORILLA by David V. Reed

D-120 **SPECIAL EFFECT** by J. F. Bone
WARLORD OF KOR by Terry Carr

ARMCHAIR SCIENCE FICTION CLASSICS, $12.95 each

C-37 **THE GREEN MAN RETURNS**
by Harold M. Sherman

C-38 **THE SHAVER MYSTERY, Book Five**
by Richard S, Shaver

C-39 **MARS CHILD**
by Cyril Judd

ARMCHAIR MASTERS OF SCIENCE FICTION SERIES, $16.95 each

MS-9 **MASTERS OF SCIENCE FICTION AND FANTASY, Vol. Nine**
Poul Anderson, "The Star Beast" and other tales

MS-10 **MASTERS OF SCIENCE FICTION, Vol. Ten**
Robert Moore Williams, "Time Tolls for Toro" and other tales

A DEEP SPACE PUBLICITY STUNT GONE WRONG

It was supposed to be an uncomplicated rocket ride to Planet Z. The talented Earth crew on board was all set to film a simple publicity stunt involving the Amelia Earhart of outer space…Gloria Kane. Kane had been the first woman to travel non-stop from Jupiter to Earth, and this adventure would take her further into the wilds of outer space than any woman had ever previously traveled. The project seemed like a surefire winner, and considering that the film company involved would get the broadcast rights for Planet Z made it worth an even bigger pile of cash. Yes, the trip to Planet Z was shaping up to be a grand idea for all involved. That is until the natives of Planet Z spread their wings and flew up to meet the incoming spacecraft. Soon the crew aboard was confronted with an abomination of horror the likes of which had never been seen before.

CAST OF CHARACTERS

LARRY LIPTON
He was the best pilot around, and looked good on camera. Little did he know his military experience would be his best asset.

GLORIA KANE
Dubbed "The Lady Daredevil" her spunk was as unmatched as her allure. But mindless torture? That was a whole 'nother deal.

GUNDAR
Fear, debauchery and vile acts were the cornerstone of this bird-man's reigning power. A power that appeared to be invincible…

"FOCUS" FORGAN
He was hotheaded and arrogant, but no one could ask for a better cameraman…or a more loyal pal.

CORONO
This exceptional man of science was needed for weapons making. But whose side would his weapons benefit?

SAVOR
He was one of the fantastic winged-warriors. Designed by Gundar, his service was ferocious.

TOM HEINE
In charge of producing the biggest televised spectacle of the year, he got exactly that…though not exactly as he'd planned it.

REVENGE OF
THE ROBOTS

By
HOWARD BROWNE
(originally writing as Lawrence Chandler)

ARMCHAIR FICTION
PO Box 4369, Medford, Oregon 97504

*For more information about Armchair Books and products, visit our
website at…*

www.armchairfiction.com

Or email us at…

armchairfiction@yahoo.com

CHAPTER ONE

LARRY LIPTON turned to see how the others were. Focus Forgan was just coming out of it. He was shaking his head in the manner of a dog getting out of a bath, and the red drops of blood kept slipping out of his nostrils and splattering the walls. Gloria Kane was still unconscious, but Larry could see the rise and fall of her breasts. The shock of entering the charged atmosphere had been worse for her than for the two men.

Larry turned again to the instrument panel, knowing it was a futile gesture. Many things had been taken into account, but certainly not this. He cursed under his breath. They were lost, at the mercy of this terrible spatial storm, blown here, thrown there, the space sphere like a balloon wholly at the mercy of the elements.

He pulled his belt in another notch and found his mind going back to the months before the flight. Not to the beginning, but right after. The months of work, research and labor that had gone into making the flight a successful one. A grunted sound, which might have been called laughter, welled in his throat. To think that man even presumed definite knowledge of the forces of the great wastes that some called outer space.

Oh, sure. The government had placed many special agents at their disposal. Had even permitted them to use the precious metal Solminum, the metal that was impervious to heat and cold; there was a ten foot thickness in the outer shell alone. Spaceweather men had been placed at their disposal, had plotted their course to take advantage of weather. The four-hundred-inch scope on Rainer had been used for three months previous to the strat of the flight, radar-electronic recording devices had measured and calculated the exact path they had to take, had looked far enough into the future for them so that they knew just what to expect. Everything had been just so-so.

He looked back at the arms and equipment locker. Three heat-energy rifles lay snugly in their cases in the locker. Thirty thousand rounds of fire power, thirty heat-energy pills, in three cases. And the pistols whose power alone could stop ten men in a tandem line. There were three of those. Then of course there were the atmosphere suits, helmets and body coverings, made of treated *Mulin,* to be worn as a precaution should their testing apparatus show a deficiency of atmosphere.

This time Larry's laugh was not forced. What the heck are you worried about he asked himself. You can only die once. A pity, though. He would have liked to know this Kane dame better. She was certainly tele-casty. A mewing sound made him turn his head quickly and his grey-green eyes met the tawny ones of Gloria Kane. She smiled, a sickly one, and whispered:

"Are we all right?"

"Right as rain," came his answer. And with it the crooked grin that Tom Heine had once called his 'sure-fire asset.'

Her eyes closed once more and Larry turned again to the pitch-blackness of outer space. And once more his thoughts went back into the past, this time to the very beginning of it all.

IT HAD started with a call to Tom Heine's office. The short, big-bellied producer was seated at his desk, the inevitable black Havana clenched tightly between his lips, his beetlebrows settled squarely over the bridge of his pudgy nose in what to others was a terrifying expression but to Larry just a comical feature, adjunct to the rest of the man.

"Larry," Heine said. "Trouble again."

Larry walked to the exercycle Heine used, mounted it and began a furious pedaling on the stationary bike.

Heine's face turned beet-red in exasperation. He got up from behind the desk and waddled over to the bike. "Damn it! Listen, Larry! Ya gotta listen!"

"Sure, Mike. Sure," Larry replied, his eyes lowered. "What's with you?"

"Don't call me Mike!" Heine howled.

"Shall we say Ike, then?" Larry said, a grin breaking on his lips. "How fast do you think I'm going?"

Heine bent his head before he was conscious he had done the other's unworded bidding. "'Bout thirty-five," he said before he could stop. "Now look," he said, sharply this time.

And Larry looked across at the other. Something in Heine's voice made him realize that whatever the movie producer had on his mind was of a serious nature. "I'm lookin' and listenin'," Larry said as he straightened.

"Okay. Grant Hayes is in his office right now waiting for an answer," Heine said. He took the cigar from between his lips, looked at it with marked disapproval—his doctor had warned him about too many of the damned things—and put it back in its corner. "Hayes says we've got to have an answer today. Says it's the biggest break we can get. And he's already in debt to the tune of a hundred thousand dollars because of it."

"That's nice," Larry said as he threw one leg over the bars and made himself more comfortable. "So break the mystery to me. Or do I have to plant my own clues? What's it all about?"

"It's all about Gloria Kane," Heine began. "'The Lady Daredevil…'"

Larry made a face of disgust. He had heard of this Kane gal. She had flown non-stop from Jupiter to Earth, the first woman in history to make the trip, though several men had done it, including Larry himself. It proved nothing except that the girl had lots of nerve and a complete disregard for her life. Larry's personal opinion was that she was headline crazy…

"…Hayes signed her to an exclusive contract," Heine went on. "Zenith Tele-cast has all rights to Miss Kane's activities for tele-casting purposes. I gotta admit the girl is tele-casty. Very. Face, figure and personality. But to get back to Hayes and the mystery. He gets the bright idea of having Miss Kane fly non-stop to Planet Z. And having the whole trip tele-cast to the states, mind you."

Larry almost fell from the exercycle from shock. To Planet Z? Why Hayes must be crazy, Larry thought. The only spaceships that had the power and authority to do that were government ships. Besides, what was the point?

HEINE HAD the answer: "There's gotta be a first to everything. He got permission from the government.

They don't care if a citizen wants to risk his or her neck. But you can't stay for more than twenty-four hours on the planet—"

"Me?" Larry howled. "Who the hell brought me into this deal?"

"I did," Heine admitted glumly. It had been such an excellent idea. Larry Lipton was a freelance to be sure. But Heine knew Larry liked working for him. So he had assumed Larry would surely take the job. He had even spoken for Larry to Hayes when the subject of relief pilot and navigator came up. Now he was no longer sure. Damn. He was going to have to put on an act. "I know, Larry," he went on in the same vein, as if no words could convey the sorrow he felt. "I opened my big yap without thinking. But can you blame me?

"You know how I've always felt about you. Haven't I always said Larry Lipton has more talent, looks, personality, than any five top-grade-telecast stars? So what does Lipton do? Stunt work!"

"Sure," Larry said. "And why not? What the heck did you want of me? I'm not interested in women mewing over me, like a tabby over a Tom. Or in having schoolgirls form clubs and naming dogs after me. I like stunt work. It pays me enough money so that I have what I want, and can get what I don't have if I *do* want it."

"That's what I mean, Larry," Heine broke in quickly. He had an idea Larry was going to get mad about the whole thing. Unless he had something else to think about. "It's been you all the time, hasn't it? Has it ever occurred to you that you may owe a debt to someone other than yourself?"

"Hey," Larry yelped. "Wait-a-minute. I don't owe a dime to anyone."

"Were we speaking of money?" Heine asked in dulcet tones. "Or is that all that's on your mind? You know we'll pay the limit..."

Larry felt shame. "Go on. And forget about money. You know I'd work for nothing if *you* asked me to, you fat Dutchman."

"...Thanks, Larry," Heine went on. His stomach warmed at the words. Larry *was* such a right guy. "You know I didn't mean that. It's just the spot the fat Dutchman is in now that bothers me. Wait, I'll explain.

"Tom Heine can go back to laying bricks and mortar and forms for concrete if this deal fails. That's right. I've sunk every dime I have and all I could borrow. If we miss, well, maybe I'll be happier being a building contractor, like in the old days."

"You couldn't be happy doing any other thing," Larry said warmly. "And you know it. Besides, you're the only honest man in the industry. We can't afford to lose you. I got it, Tom. See how right I am. Hayes got permission from the F. C. C. to use their exclusive tele-wave pattern from Planet Z to the Earth. In twenty-four hours we can show the whole planet, and get the tele-cast copyright. There'll be a fortune in it, all right. Sure. That's it. With Planet Z as the outside station between Earth and all outer space it has a tremendous importance to us, especially since they intercepted signals from the mystery planet in the dark nebulae beyond Orion. The papers were full of it ten months ago.

"Then Venus intercepted some signals. And after that we didn't get a thing, until we discovered Planet Z and found that they were in a perfect spot for reception. And that's why the government clamped down on all space travel to the planet. I'm just curious as to how Hayes got permission."

HEINE HAD been listening in downright admiration. Larry had figured the thing out, but exactly. And he was right. "Well, it seems that Hayes got in on the ground floor because of the educational end of the tele-cast. We get the copyright for three years for purposes of education. After, we can use the copyright to any purpose we see fit. Which still makes it a terrific deal. Right?"

"And how."

"So, let's go to Hayes' office and tell him you're in on the deal. You, 'Focus' Forgan and Miss Kane."

"Focus Forgan," Larry growled and gave up. If there was a man he disliked, it was Forgan. Loud, a drinker, a man-with-the-women sort of character who had a way with a tele-camera. Larry hated the other's guts. And Heine knew it. But Forgan was the best man in the business and Hayes was interested only in getting results. Personal enmities had no place in their project, Hayes had said. Those were Tom Heine's words, after Larry blew his top.

"Okay," Larry said. "Might as well get it over with. Let's go."

"Fine. Fine." Heine was affability itself, as they started off. "Besides, you'll get to meet Miss Kane. She's there too."

Larry looked with interest at the woman who was

standing by the side of Frederick Hayes. They had their backs to the two who had entered, and Hayes was deep in explanation of a blueprint on the wall. They turned as Heine cleared his throat and Hayes smiled his thin-lipped banker's smile at the two men. He was a tall man, slender, severely though impeccably dressed, with a taste for dark suits and imported shirts. He had a narrow, well-groomed face, whose predominating features were a pair of steel-grey eyes that had authority in them. Hayes was a fighter. And between him and Heine they had built Zenith Tele-cast to the apex of the business.

But Larry had seen Hayes before. It was the woman who held his attention. If this was Gloria Kane she was all Tom Heine had said. What was more, she knew how to dress. Tailored clothes of good taste and cut showed her figure to perfection. She did not affect bangles and spangles as other women did, nor were her fingers adorned with rings. He noticed in passing that there was no marriage band on her finger. And smiled within him that he should notice it.

"Well," Hayes' voice boomed in bass tones. "So you've brought Larry along. Good, Tom. Now, Miss Kane, I want to introduce Larry Lipton, your co-pilot and navigator. Larry, Gloria Kane—"

She thrust a hand out and Larry took it, and felt the strength of her fingers in the sudden nervous grip she gave him.

"Delighted, Larry," she said. "I've heard about you. All to the good."

"Yeah?" Larry's voice was a needle-sharp lance. "I heard about you too. You're pretty good, the papers say."

He didn't quite know why he said what he did. He knew it sounded bad, and certainly there hadn't been any call for his sarcasm. But she should have acted otherwise, and not been so pleasant.

"Look, buster," her voice matched his, only her's was a shade colder. "I don't want any trouble and I'm not looking for any. This wasn't my idea; it was Hayes here. And if I'm going to have some sky-cowboy acting cutely jealous because a woman's got the important end of this flight, he can go chase kites. You're not the only man can navigate. So get this straight. You'll either take orders from me or you can forget the invitation you've had to join up."

"Sorry, Miss Kane," Larry's voice held icicles in it. "Guess I talked out of turn. It won't happen again."

SHE SMILED, trying to break the ice. "That's all right. Lordy. A man's entitled to a mad once in a while. I know I blow up sometimes when... Okay. We'll forget it." She had seen his eyes remained immune to her plea though his lips shaped a silly grin. "Here, Mister Lipton. Take a look at this."

She pointed to the blueprint on the wall. Larry moved to her side and became aware that she also knew how to apply perfume. It was such a clean odor, with a fragrance that barely made itself felt. He liked it. Then Hayes' voice was explaining the blueprint:

"Grove Aeronautic Inc. are making the space sphere for us. The inner shell is complete. The government is letting us use enough Solminum for a ten-foot-thick outer shell. In a week you, Miss Kane and Forgan will go to Mt. Rainier to the observatory where you'll brief up on weather for the trip. By the time you return we'll be about ready for a test flight. How does that strike you?"

"It's okay with me," Larry said.

They parted on that note.

And three months to the day, the space sphere was in readiness. Larry would rather have started without the usual Hollywood trimmings. But it was only good publicity to have photographers, writers from magazines, feature men from the news syndicates, and government officials at the takeoff. Larry hated it. But Gloria Kane seemed to revel in it. As for Focus Forgan, he mugged as if the whole thing had been planned solely for him.

Then the shooting ended, the newsmen and magazine feature writers took their last notes, Gloria stepped within the sphere and Larry flipped the switch that closed the hatch, and in a moment Gloria took the controls. There was an expectant hush, a smile from the girl, and they were off.

Larry was in the co-pilot's seat, Gloria was at the controls, and Forgan had a seat, which had been built especially for him, where he could always be at the tele-camera. For, from the very beginning, the flight was on the tele-waves.

Forgan was a roughneck. He looked like it, acted like it, and talked like it. He had a thick, muscular body, a face that was heavily fleshed, with a broken nose, a memento of the days when he fought for a living, and a shock of heavy red hair.

It was strange, but there had been no trouble from Forgan at the observatory. It was evident that Hayes had talked to the man and had warned him about making trouble. Yet Forgan made no bones about his dislike. It was just that he wasn't too obvious. Rather it was in his complete indifference to Larry that the co-pilot felt resentful. In fact up to the very last minute Forgan kept the peace. But once the hatch was closed and they were off he changed.

"Well, pretty boy," Forgan said, turning his head in Larry's direction. "This thing ought to payoff pretty good for you, pretty darned good."

"What do you mean, bird-brain?" Larry asked.

"A cinch. Zenith Tele-cast grooms Pretty-boy Lipton for feature roles on the strength of this. Don't forget, you televise just like an angel. Or that's what the gals say."

OH, OH, LARRY thought. So Forgan had been saving his cracks just for now. He kept a tight grip on himself. But not the girl. She had the controls on automatic so she could talk without paying any attention to the panel.

"What's this, Forgan?" she asked.

"Y'mean you didn't know?" Forgan dug it deep. "That this guy's Tom Heine's boy. Sure. The whole thing's just a publicity gag. Lipton's gonna get all the…"

"That's a lie, mug," Larry spat between his teeth. "And you know it."

Forgan's shoulders heaved in a shrug. He slapped his palms together and laughed. "So I'm a liar. But how come they got good-looking for navigator and co-pilot? There must be a dozen guys who've space-traveled. Why Lipton?"

"Maybe he was the best obtainable?" Gloria said.

"Hah! That's a laugh. The best four-flusher," Forgan growled.

Larry slipped free of the belt, leaped out of the seat and ran to Forgan's side.

"Get out of there, you ape, and I'll show you some four-flushing. Come on!" he yelled.

Forgan's eyes gleamed in delight. He had hoped the needle would make Lipton break. He'd been wanting to slap that pretty face around for a long while. And now he was going to. But he didn't.

"That'll be enough," the girl's voice bit at them. "What the devil do you two think you're doing? I've heard about you two. *So get this:* Save your brawling for the time when we get back. There'll be none of it aboard ship. I'm still boss. One more crack from you, Forgan, and I'll radio for help. I swear it. As for you, Lipton, keep that temper of yours down. I didn't like it when first I heard it and I like it less now. That's all we need, a fight, and this whole trip will blow high as a weather kite…"

Larry's fists were still clenched as he turned and went back to his seat. But the light of reason had returned to his eyes and his brain was hitting on all cylinders. Of course she was right. He should have never allowed Forgan's deliberate needle to penetrate his hide. He manufactured a grin and a quip:

"If you radio for help, someone's liable to say, 'What's the matter, can't you square the billing?'"

BUT SHE wasn't smiling. "Look, Larry," she said. "Let's not talk about billing or tele-casting anymore. What you could do is give me a little information about this Planet Z."

"Hmm... There isn't a heck of a lot to tell. It was first observed a couple of years ago—let me see—'81 to be exact. It is, by a long ways, the furthest planet from the sun. I don't know its physical dimensions, but it is the smallest of them all, perhaps half the size of Mercury. No satellites, atmosphere about like Venus, some sort of life but none so complex and varied as we have, though there are creatures of the subhuman species.

"It is what is called a dark planet; it reflects no light for some unexplained reason. But it emits certain rays akin to the cosmic cycle, and it acts for perfect reception for the signals from the nebulae beyond Orion. And that, chillun, is about all I know."

"Thank you, professor," she said lightly. "But the course is not quite complete. What about that magnetic field they told us of at the observatory?"

"Oh, that." He pretended it was nothing. "I thought you understood? Well, it seems all the planets have a magnetic field. Planet Z has a patterned field. So on our flight map the weather boys laid out minute instructions for approach and landing. And since it might be on your mind as to why they suggested I bring the ship in for a landing, it is because of the magnetic field. I have flown through such fields. When they asked you about landings on Venus and Mercury, you said you hadn't flown to those. Those two planets have similar patterns. So, naturally, they suggested I bring the ship in."

It *had* been on her mind. Now she understood and felt better about it. This time when she smiled, her lips seemed to beg forgiveness that she had felt the way she did about it. He winked at her and turned to the instrument panel again, as if to close the incident.

Forgan had been listening closely. He had to admit a grudging admiration of Larry's knowledge, small though it was. Yet, at Rainier, they had treated him with respect. Oh, Lipton wasn't really a four-flusher. It was just that sometimes the man irritated Forgan. The cameraman went back to his built-in booth and began to tele-cast...

CHAPTER TWO

THEY WERE a full day beyond Venus when first Larry noticed something was wrong. Gloria was asleep, as was Forgan. Larry was at the controls, giving them an automatic check-up. They had been set at the start but the check-up was one of his duties. His glance traveled past the pilot control and went back to it. Something had caught his eye... His brow knit when he saw what was wrong. The needle was moving in jerks back and forth away from the set-point. It didn't cause him any worry. Just that real work was to be involved if the gauge was wrong. Gloria and he would have to spell each other on manual. He took it off automatic and used his hands. And the furrow deepened on his brow. The pilot was not working at all; the needle continued its variations to either side of set-point.

He leaned back and tried to figure out the cause. But after a moment he gave up, simply because there were too many places in which the trouble might lie. He fished his nav. maps from the drawer, studied them for a while for orientation and set the manuals on. Then he set his course. Only the controls didn't work that way either. And that meant *real* trouble. The ship was just out of control. He tried everything and nothing worked; he could not rudder it one way or another, he could not gain speed or decrease it, he could do nothing but fiddle with the levers and buttons on the panel, like an infant with a complex set of blocks. And with as little chance of accomplishing anything structural.

He pulled the hand mike out and awakened the girl and Forgan and asked them forward. Forgan was rubbing the sleep from his eyes, growling that it was a hell of a time to call someone, just when sleep was beginning to feel good. But one look at Larry's face and Gloria shut the cameraman up.

"How bad is it?" she asked.

Larry liked that. No silly questions as to what happened. Just a sensible question.

"Pretty bad. Controls are shot."

She paled beneath the tanned skin. But her voice held not the faintest tremor of fear. "We have clearance past Venus so they'll be on the lookout for us. I don't like doing this but—I guess we'll have to radio for help. Darn it." Her voice held an edge of tears.

"Yeah," Larry said. "We have clearance so they'll be watching and giving us room. Trouble is we're going at such speed we're liable to bust right through the freight air lanes, which could mean a collision with one of those sky box cars. Well, you're the boss. Radio it'll have to be."

And for once Forgan had no wisecrack.

Larry opened the channel to Venus and began a monotonous and steady call. But after a full minute of it he switched to the Earth channel. He called the beam

113

for perhaps thirty seconds, then switched off altogether. "We're not getting through and I can't raise them. So let's face it. It's in the lap of the gods."

ANOTHER DAY went by. The space sphere sped through the impenetrable darkness of space with a speed close to that of light. Within, the three occupants whiled away their time at cards, food and talk. Somehow they managed to stay out of the freight lanes, Larry, keeping a constant watch on the course the ship was pursuing, became convinced of a strange thing. He did not communicate his suspicions to either of his companions. But he had more than just an idea that the ship was taking a definite, though mysterious course for an unknown destination. They were going to pass Planet Z by a hundred million miles…

Then, at the beginning of the third twenty-four hours, the spacial storm struck. Gloria was at the controls, writing a letter on the panel. Forgan was taking a catnap and Larry was listening to a recording of the Eroica. It was as if all controls had been taken away from the huge sphere. Larry compared what happened to an incident he had known on a *Star* class sailboat on Lake Michigan when a sudden squall struck.

A thousand needles seemed to have struck him all at the same time. The room was charged with the stuff. He gritted his teeth and waited for the first shock to pass. He knew there would be others. He tried to move, to get to the girl, but he could not move a single muscle, not even those of the voice box. Another shock and a third. Each a little less numbing. He felt drained of all feeling after the third. But that one was also the last.

He pulled himself away from the machine and staggered forward on clumsily moving legs. He had to see how Gloria was. He saw her hanging limply against the strap. But she was alive. He could see the cloth move slowly across the shoulders as she breathed shallowly. Then the first buffeting blow struck and knocked him sprawling forward. Fortunately the first shock was a light one. He managed to strap himself in. And Forgan crashed into the compartment, bellowing:

"What the hell's the matter, Prettyboy? Who's shooting needles at us?"

The second crashing shock knocked him against the edge of the instrument panel. His face hit with a sickening thud and Forgan rolled to the floor. Larry slipped out of his belt, ran to Forgan's side and made him fast in his own chair, then returned to his own seat. The strap held him fast, but it seemed to Larry that his insides were tearing loose as the ship spun on its axis, dove and climbed like some possessed thing. He could see through the pilot's port that they were in the midst of a hail of solid particles, too many to count, yet each one solid as hail.

And as quickly as the strange storm struck, so quickly did it die. All this went through his mind. Now what?

HE LOOKED around and saw Gloria's eyes open, heard her ask, "Are we all right?" and saw her eyes close again. Forgan, too, was coming out of it, shaking his head back and forth, the blood dripping from his nose to spatter the walls. Then the bloodshot eyes opened wide and a snarl curled his lip.

"What the hell?" he asked weakly. "Hey! What happened?"

Larry undid his strap, stepped weakly forward and helped Forgan undo his. "I don't know, Focus," Larry said. "I just don't know. But I think we're through it. Miss Kane's out. Let's get her to her sleeping quarters."

But she was fully conscious as they stepped to her side. She shook her head when they wanted to undo the strap. "I—I'm all right," she said weakly. "Just give me a minute or so. Whew. I hope we don't have to go through that any more."

"Amen," Forgan said.

"I don't know," Larry said. "But I think we've passed through the worst of it. Hmm. That was something the meteorologists didn't warn us about." He looked abstractedly at the instrument panel. The pilot needle caught his eye. It was showing a true course without a quiver. "Gloria! Focus! Look. It's working again."

The three crowded close to the panel and watched it for a second or so. Then Larry seated himself at the panel and began to work out the formula of distance and speed. His eyes were wide in disbelief when he turned to them at last.

"We're going back to Planet Z. But not to the port the government has. To the opposite side."

"So what?" Focus asked. "So long as we get there and I can get some real shots."

"Aah!" Larry was disgusted. "You don't understand. Our path was plotted. Now we're on our own."

And again Forgan asked, "So what? Ain't you a pilot? If you ain't so let Miss Kane take over."

Gloria hid a grin under a palm. She felt like laughing

but was afraid the sound would be mistaken for hysteria. Instead, she said:

"It's all right, Focus, Larry can bring us in. And *I* know what he means. But one thing I'm grateful for. We're definitely going to hit our goal."

LARRY BRAKED down until he was at landing speed. They were skimming the ground at some thousand feet altitude. Below, as if it was an Earth scene, green-clad hills stretched to the horizon. Here and there Larry saw open grassy ground. Then he saw a stretch large enough for a landing and called that he was coming in…

"Better use the atmosphere suits," Larry suggested. "And let's not take any chances. We'll take along the heat-pistols."

The man and woman nodded in agreement and, after dressing in the *Mulin* treated garments, Focus broke out the pistols and ten rounds of heat-energy caps. Then Larry opened the Intel and the three stepped out into broad daylight.

Gloria's voice, muffled by the head plate, came to him:

"Now isn't this silly. If there's plant life, there's the same atmosphere as on the Earth."

She was already undoing the outside buckles. In a moment she stepped out of the suit and after another moment the two men followed her lead. Forgan was shaking his in disgust.

"Aah! Always wants to play boss," he said. "Hey, pretty-boy. Why don't you let the dame show the way?"

"Why don't you mind your own moronic business?"

Larry asked in irritation.

Forgan reddened, dropped the suit to the ground and leaped forward. His left flashed in a hook to the side of Larry's jaw, and as Larry fell from the blow his right came up hard. But Larry ducked in time, though his head seemed to be spinning like a top. He could hear Gloria's horrified yelling as from a distance. But this time he and Focus were going to settle things.

He ducked a jab, another, and sent a looping left to Focus' nose. It stopped the heavier man. But Forgan only burrowed his head between his shoulders and charged forward, his fists pumping like pistons. But Larry was far the better boxer and he parried and ducked the blows with ease. Three times he chopped short punches to the side of Forgan's face and three times the other staggered. Then he rolled with the fourth and shot a counter full on the button. It knocked Larry off his feet.

There were three suns, Larry decided. Then how come there were four Forgans? And two Glorias? Something was wrong somewhere. He could hear someone asking him to, "Get up. And I'll knock you all the way back to Chicago," but he couldn't understand why. He didn't want to go to Chicago. If any place, he preferred Hollywood. Or even better, New York. Why Chicago?

Then someone was pulling at his arm and he jerked it out of the someone's hold. He heard a startled sound of dismay, a feminine one, and snapped out of his daze. Gloria was sitting on the ground, facing him. Her face was red all the way to her eyes. And those blazed in blinding anger.

"YOU—you stinker!" she wailed. "You struck me!"

He scrambled erect, forgetting Forgan and everything else and rushed forward and helped her to her feet. "I'm sorry," he said.

"Yeah," she groaned. "You look so different when you're sorry."

Anger gripped him again. "Then why the devil did you interfere? Why can't you just be a woman and let the men do the men's work? But no! You've got to show your femininity. So you get hurt! Serves you right."

HER FACE drained of color at his biting words. She rose, and smiling, strode toward him. It was an enigmatic smile, and he was curious as to its meaning. His reflex block of the sudden slap she gave him was a bit slow. His face burned at the mark her five fingers left on it. But his smile matched hers.

"Not for your words," she said. "But for your ego. Perhaps it won't be so great, now?"

"Not him, Miss Kane," a voice bellowed. "He's the greatest flyer, the greatest lover, the greatest guy in the whole world. This or any other world."

They turned at the unexpected sound and saw Focus Forgan, hands on hips, head thrown back, laughing uproariously.

But the girl did not find either the man or his words amusing. She strode toward him and he retreated at the look on her face, his own reflecting dismay. "Now, Miss Kane," he cautioned. "I didn't mean anythin'…"

She was intent on what she was doing. Forgan had his back to the approaching creatures, so only Larry

Lipton saw them. They were still some way off. But his keen sight had seen them in the distance.

"Gloria, Focus!" he called in warning. "Down! Quick!"

They obeyed on the instant, the urgency in his tone a command they knew better than to disobey. The grass was high and covered them completely. Larry crawled forward, calling as he did, "Get your guns out."

Forgan and the girl were close together when Larry reached them. "I don't know whether they saw us or not," Larry said in a whisper. "But I'm sure they're not the people from the government station."

"How far off were they?" Gloria asked.

"About a quarter mile."

"So what's all this for?" Focus asked. "Maybe they're friends? What the heck? We got the power right here," he patted his heat-pistol. "If they get smart so we bump them."

There was something in what Forgan said, Larry thought. Yet he had the strangest feeling that the strangers were not friends—that they held a definite threat for the three from Earth. "Wel-ll. Maybe you're right, Focus. But it won't hurt to just wait here and see what they look like. If they look like they're friendly *then* we can show ourselves. How do you feel about it Gloria?"

I feel like an idiot, she thought. "I've always hated discretion," she said. "But in this case..." She had hated to say what she did, but Larry had forced her into a corner. Her real feelings matched Forgan's. If they weren't friendly, why the heat-pistols would even the odds. But an instant's reflection made Larry's plan the better. Maybe they had weapons equal to the Earth people's? If so… She became grim at the thought. Their position then was not an enviable one.

The three peered over the knee-high grass toward the large group of beings approaching, with mixed feelings.

THERE WAS something not quite human about those people, Larry decided. Yet he could not figure out why. They walked erect, and even at the distance which separated them, he could make out that they had but two legs and arms and but one head. They were not comic-strip characters. He was sure of that. Until they were some hundred yards removed. Then he changed his mind.

The human beings he knew had no wings sprouting from their shoulder blades.

His companions saw what he did at the same time.

"Jeez," Forgan grunted. "I didn't know Heaven was like this."

"Don't be funny," the girl said, her eyes intent on the approaching strangers. "But other than their having wings, they look all right to me."

"Think we ought to risk it?" Larry asked.

"Yes. But let's be careful and keep our fingers close to the trigger pull."

They were about to suit the action to the words when something happened that changed their minds. They had forgotten about the space sphere. It was lying out there in the meadow, an immense sphere of gleaming Solminum. It proved to be the goal.

Larry hadn't been sure the things attached to these beings' shoulders were wings. He was certain in a very short while. The whole group suddenly took wing, like a group of fabulously large geese, and flew straight up until they were quite a distance above the sphere. Then, much like the old-time planes the air force used, they peeled off, one by one, and dived straight down at the sphere.

The huge wings beat too swiftly for the eye to follow, and their speed was so low it didn't seem possible they would miss. Larry counted them as they came in. Sixty-two. He watched them as they flew to one side, then gasped audibly as they rose straight up again and dove once more. His gasp was echoed by the others as they watched. For this time there was a difference. They could not see what the bird-men did; their movements were too fast, but they could see the results. Tiny puffs of smoke touched the sphere as each passed. The whole ship seemed to be shrouded in the smoke. Then, as if from internal combustion, the sphere burst into flames.

It was impossible! Larry knew it. It just couldn't be. The thing was constructed of Solminum. Heat-resistant to such an extant it could withstand the tremendous heat of outer space, yet whatever means these bird-like creatures used generated an energy beyond the power of human conception.

It was over quickly. Not even ashes to mark the grave of the space sphere...

Larry rose, shoulders drooping. The girl and Forgan followed his example. And for once the irrepressible Forgan had nothing to say. Gloria spoke for all, her voice low, filled with horror:

"They're monsters. How could they know if there was anyone in the ship?"

"They didn't," Larry said. "So they took no chances. It's just common sense to destroy what you don't trust."

Forgan voiced the question lying at the bottom of their hearts, "So that's over. But what about us? What do we do now? No radio, no tele-cast camera, no way of letting the home folks know what's happened. Anybody got an answer?"

"Not at the moment," Larry said. He knew, however, that inaction would cripple them, let the seeds of fear eat at them, would soon make them fly at each other's throats and in the end force them into actions over which they could have no control. "But this I do know," he went on. "That we just can't stay here.

"Suppose we sit down and sort of map a near future for us?"

FORGAN LOOKED at the girl, his beetlebrows furrowed in thought, and Gloria looked at him. They nodded simultaneously and turned to Larry, who was already falling to the ground.

"Okay, Lipton," Forgan said. "Let's hear your angle. Then maybe Miss Kane'll have something to add, and maybe even me. Shoot."

"Well, first, I think that there isn't any more government station. These bird-people have control of it now. But the installations might be there. That's for one. For another, and what may prove to be our best bet, these beings have exhibited a knowledge that shows they're thinking beings. So they must have cities, places of habitation. I say best bet because we might find them friendly if we show that they have nothing to fear from, us.

"But there is one thing that puzzles me. This is supposed to be a dark planet. Yet if we look above there is definitely light, though from what source puzzles me because there is no sun. Now, if you remember our orientation, we were told that the whole planet was dark, though not cold, because we were not told to take clothes other than the ones we wore. So I must come to this conclusion. That we did not reach our goal after all."

"I don't get it, buster," Forgan said. "First you say we did then you say we didn't. And don't give me the old double-talk. Because only a couple of seconds ago you said you didn't think the government station was there any more. Right?"

"Forgan's right, Larry," Gloria said. "I'm curious also."

"It's rather simple," Larry explained smilingly. "If you remember, we were on a constant beam with the station. But we never got in contact. We were told we wouldn't until we reached the limits of their wavelength. But even when we were in that limit we received no signals. Therefore, to bring my dialectic discussion to a summary and logical conclusion, the station is no longer in operation. And, to add two and two together, since this planet is obviously not dark, we never landed on the one we aimed for, altogether."

"Y'know," Forgan said, admiration in his voice despite him, "the boy's right. It all makes sense."

"Except for one thing," Gloria pointed out. "What has this place to do with the other, although Mister Lipton thinks that the two are related?"

"Because our instruments *were* working just before we

landed. And they pointed to the fact we had reached our goal. Positively. It's my idea that this thing is a sort of satellite of the dark planets. And, for some reason, has never been reported. Unless—"

"Unless what?" Gloria leaned forward, her vivid eyes wide, and her lovely face alight with interest.

"—Unless," Larry continued, "our boys never sent any of the messages back to Earth at all."

Forgan grunted. "You're nuts, guy!" he exploded. "How could that be?"

"Simple. If they were smart enough to invent a weapon they were able to carry, yet one which made nothing of something as large as the spaceship, then they could quite easily have taken over the installations and no one would be the wiser."

"And Larry's right," Gloria said.

"So he's right," Forgan said. "And now what do we do?"

"Anything but just sit here. For one thing, what about food? And for another, since there isn't any sun, there won't be night. Which brings up the business of sleep," Gloria said. "Although it really has no bearing on anything, I realize."

"Well, there was one important thing you mentioned," Larry said. "Food. So just let's get up and go. It doesn't make any difference which way. One will do as well as the next."

LARRY TOOK the lead, and Forgan brought up the rear. The light, mysterious though pleasant, was strange since there were no shadows. There were no trees though there were some fairly tall hedge-like bushes.

There seemed a complete absence of animal life. The countryside was rolling and hilly and time meant nothing since the light was constant, and as they walked, they talked, though they kept a constant watch for the bird-like creatures.

Several hours must have passed before Gloria voiced a hunger plaint.

"I got a piece of gum, Miss Kane. Ain't much but maybe it'll help," Forgan said.

She took it, grateful for the small bit of satisfaction it would give.

Larry had seen that the hedges had grown thicker, more frequent as they walked along. More, as time went by he became aware of something that he had noticed from the beginning, but to which he had paid small attention. There were an immense number of birds, though all seemed voiceless. And these birds seemed to be following them in their march. It was strange to see these vari-colored flyers, small and large, skimming the hedges and returning to sometimes fly just above their heads, each lovely to see and each voiceless.

They came at last to an impasse. The hedges stretched in a long straight line before them, an impenetrable wall of brush. Larry scratched at his head, wondering what to do. They had very little choice. It was either through the hedges or follow the curving line. He looked at Forgan and the cameraman could only shrug. As for Gloria, she was beginning to feel tiredness now as well as hunger.

"Think you can manage, Gloria?" Larry asked, gesturing toward the hedges.

"I suppose," the girl said wearily. "Maybe we'll find

something on the other side."

"Yeah," Forgan supplemented. "I'm getting kinda tired of this scenery."

Larry turned his head to see if he could spot a path that might lead through, but though he could see light there was no definition that showed a pattern. Gotta risk it, he thought. He sent a silent prayer skyward as he started forward, hoping that it would find the right ear.

The branches bent with his body and he felt a thankfulness it was not a thorn hedge. The branches were rubbery rather than stiff. They broke through with a suddenness that startled, and what Larry saw made him fall swiftly on his face. The trouble was the others were close behind, and not so swift in their reflexes.

"Damn," Larry muttered as he rose and stepped in front of the girl. "Now we're in for it."

CHAPTER THREE

THEY HAD come on a roadway, wide, smooth and well traveled. Or at least for the moment. A long line of two-wheeled vehicles was passing. These affairs were about twenty feet long, and shaped somewhat like a shallow boat. Seated in each were perhaps fifty of the bird-men. They were dressed in flesh-colored coveralls. Their heads were bare and well shaped. At their waists a tube-like gadget hung suspended from a belt. All this Larry saw before one of the bird-men spotted them as the two-wheeler passed them. As he turned and called attention to them to his companions, Larry rose and stepped in front of the girl.

"First guy makes a wrong move I'm blasting," Forgan

said in an aside.

"Better not. Make sure first," Larry cautioned.

But it was Gloria who gave the most sensible advice: "Better put those pistols back," she said. "And let's just put our hands up in the air. They may not know what it means, but they can't mistake it for truculence."

The long line of vehicles had stopped, as if some strange and silent signal had been given. And as some of the bird-men leaped from their positions, others spread their wings and flew toward the three at the side of the road, to hover above them with a great flapping of wings.

Now the three Earth people had a close look at the bird people. They looked human in every way, other than the wings that seemed to grow from the shoulder blades. At least the appearance was thus, the coveralls hiding the joint. A slit had been made in the garment, permitting the feathered wing complete freedom.

"What do you do here?" the first to reach them asked in low, well-modulated tones.

"Why, they speak English," Gloria said, her voice shrill with surprise.

The man smiled and they saw his teeth were white and even. "We speak the Universal tongue," he said. "But my question needs answering."

"We flew here in the sphere you people burned," Larry said.

They were completely surrounded now. They could feel the curiosity of these bird people, feel it in the studied glances and low whispers which reached their ears.

"Oh-h. I see. Well, come along then…"

He turned and marched back to the vehicle without a second glance to see whether they were following or not. But Larry noticed that the ones in the air did not fly back, but kept up the hovering directly over their heads.

"Shall we go, kiddies?" Forgan asked, his mouth twisted in a crooked grin.

"Guess the choice isn't ours," Gloria said as she took the lead.

Room was made for them in the vehicle of the one who had questioned them and the lone line started off again. The pace was rather leisurely but now there were some from every two-wheeler who flew above as if in escort. Pretty smart, Larry thought to himself. Maybe they figure there are more of us. I just wish there were. Quite suddenly he felt, as if it were a physical thing, the burning stare of someone behind him.

"It would do no good," a voice whispered.

"What wouldn't?" Larry asked.

Forgan and the girl turned toward him, their eyes wide in silent questioning.

"Your having allies," the bird-man said. He smiled pleasantly and Larry really noticed that the man's face was even-featured, with nicely proportioned nose, mouth and eyes. The hands were large though well shaped, and the fingers showed sensitivity in their length.

"So you read my mind?" Larry asked.

"A not too difficult thing," the other answered. "You will learn to control your thinking better."

"By the way," Larry asked. "Where are we going?"

"To Koba," the other replied. "The city of our people. It will not be long."

SO THEY have cities, Larry thought. And stopped thinking. Perhaps it was better not to think. He turned away and looked over the rail against which he leaned. He noticed that the bird-men overhead were no longer there. They had come in to their respective cars.

"Larry," Gloria's voice, muted in amazement, called him out of his revere. "Look..."

He turned in the direction of her gaze and whistled under his breath. The spires of hundreds of buildings showed low on the horizon. His distance-trained eyes told him that those spires must reach thousands of feet into the air. As if the sight of the city of Koba made itself felt in a strange fashion the cavalcade of two-wheeler's speeded up their pace. They seemed to skim the surface of the road.

"Whew," Forgan whistled. "These things can really travel. Man! We must be going a hundred miles an hour."

But Larry had eyes only for the city, coming closer by the second. He could see spider-webs of girders connecting the buildings. Then, as they reached a point where the perspective showed them in all their majesty, he realized their immensity. There were thousands of them. And now they came to parallel roads, and cross roads. Traffic lights blossomed overhead. There were all sorts of vehicles to be seen, all travelling at a terrific clip. But the large two-wheelers had the right-of-way.

Then they were on a sort of bridge, a bridge that had no supports. Built on thin air. Larry wondered how it held their weight. He turned to see whether the bird-man would answer his unspoken question but the other seemed lost in thoughts of his own. Ruefully, Larry wished he had the faculty of reading minds. Many questions would surely have been answered.

Now they were definitely off the ground. And their speed increased, the closer they got to Koba. They were going so fast everything was a blur. And then they were among the buildings. Suddenly the light was no longer there. Darkness closed in on them. Gloria stifled a scream. Larry put his arm about her instinctively in a protective gesture. And she snuggled in its strength.

"Do not fear," a voice said comfortingly. "We are but approaching our goal. Soon we will be there."

They braked to a stop that brought a murmur of admiration from Forgan. At the speed they had been going he had been wondering how far they'd have to travel before coming to a stop. A matter of seconds. And the wonder of it was that they did not slam forward as he had thought they would.

"Follow us, please," said the bird-man who had first spoken to them. He seemed to be a leader of sorts, though there was nothing in either his dress or manner that differentiated him from the others.

A soft, mellow glow enveloped them. They were in an immense hall, the walls of which shed this light. The entire crew, other than the man who was leading them, stepped into an open elevator that was at the landing. Gloria and her companions followed in the footsteps of the bird-man. They walked for a distance of perhaps a quarter of a mile along the immense corridor. Now and then other corridors bisected theirs. But they seemed the only ones abroad.

FINALLY they reached another elevator, one in a

bank of three. The others were also open, as if waiting the arrival of passengers. The four stepped within the, huge cage, built to hold hundreds of people, and without warning the thing started upward. Larry couldn't understand how it worked; no one was at the controls. For one thing there were no controls, and for another, there was the faintest sound of machinery at work. Other than the first sound there were no further ones. And in a second or two the huge doors slid open and they stepped out.

"No-o," Forgan said aloud.

Larry and the girl understood exactly what he meant.

They were in a sort of birdcage. It was the only way to describe it. But the thing was hundreds of feet high, and fully two hundred feet across. There were great swinging bars on which were perched *millions* of birds, little ones. The sound of their trilling was deafening in this closed space.

"Silence, oh birds of Koba," their guide shouted. "I bring you people of another world."

The sudden silence that followed his shout was terrifying. Larry felt his hair prickle and felt Gloria suddenly press close to him. His throat was suddenly dry and from the corner of his eye he saw Forgan go pale. Yet there was no reason he could lay hands to why he felt this terror.

A single bird fluttered close on slowly moving wings. Closer and closer it came until it passed before them in slow revue. Larry wanted to close his eyes, to look aside, to see anything other than what he was seeing. The tiny bird, maybe five inches from the tip of its beak to the furthest tail feather, had the face of a man. An old face, an evil face, a face that held all the marks of evil incarnate.

"What kind of a hell is this?" Forgan's hoarse whisper reached Larry as from a distance.

But Larry had eyes and ears only for the bird that was flying back before them again.

"Fine. Fine," came a tiny piping voice from the throat of the bird. "Very good, Savor. I like these. Where are they from?"

"Answer!" Savor shouted at them.

Larry swallowed the cottony saliva and said: "From a planet called Earth."

"Aie! Earth, eh? Yes, ye-es. Heard of it. Ninth cycle planet. Hmm! We have come a long way. But the Venusians told us that it was on Earth we would find the nesting grounds we have been seeking for all these millennia. So then...

"I see the sexes are mixed. Good. Propagation is a means for our ends also. Now then. How did you arrive on this space island? As the others did from the dark planet? In the same kind of space vehicle?"

Larry remained silent. A child's laugh came from the throat of the bird fluttering on swiftly moving wings before him.

"Emotionally disturbed, isn't he? To be expected, Savor. Take him and the others to the room of memory. And let me know what you learn."

"Shall I bust this goon one?" Forgan asked as Savor held the doors to the huge birdcage open. There was a strange smile on the man's face, a smile that seemed to invite violence. Larry interpreted it correctly, and decided he would be the one to test it, not Forgan.

"Nope. Not yet, anyway," Larry said aloud, and deliberately smiled into the other's eyes. Forgan worried his brow about the grin, but held his peace.

SAVOR FOLLOWED them out, then stepped briskly to the fore. His steps and the other's echoed hollowly on the marble flagstones. Not a person was to be seen as they walked the interminable length of the corridor. And when they arrived at their goal it was with the same unexpectedness as when they came to the gigantic bird cage.

They finally came to the end of the corridor, and there, at the very turn, was an immense nail-studded door. Savor simply stood before it and it opened wide to him. The three earth people could only stare open-mouthed at what was before them. Fully a hundred men were busily engaged in some sort of work in the large room. One of them, a tall lean man, with a saturnine look about the eyes and mouth, came forward. Larry was quick to note that this man was wingless.

"Aah! Savor, the warrior. What brings you now?"

"These," Savor said severely. It was apparent he and the other shared the same opinions about each other. Larry filed away their mutual dislike for future reference. "Earth people," Savor continued. "The same miserable creatures we found on the dark planet."

"Not too miserable," the man in the smock said. "Fact of the matter was there were one or two who were highly intelligent. Too bad the military wanted them. But, we must remember our mission, mustn't we?"

Savor's face went crimson. His lips thinned into a bloodless line. Angry words were on the tip of his tongue, but he drew them back.

"It would be well to bear it in mind. That and nothing else. But I have no time for idle talk. The bird-man wants these placed in the memory machine and their reactions recorded. I must report back."

"But of course," the other said, then pursed his lips. "The *bird-man* wants their memory reactions. Very well. Find a seat somewhere, and be careful where. We're working at something very deadly. The smallest drop would kill—"

Savor's face blanched. "Ah, no, thank you. I'll stand."

"As you wish," the other said. "And now, good people, will you follow me."

He led them into another, smaller room, one which held a single complicated piece of machinery. A seat was at one, before which was the same sort of apparatus an optometrist uses to peer into patients' eyes.

"The lady first, if you don't mind?" the saturnine-faced man said.

"Not at all," Larry said. Forgan merely grunted.

"Thank you. Now let me place this eyepiece at the proper level—so—now! Just look at the crosspiece for a moment... Savor is such a bore. It is no longer fun to bait him, even. Now you look like a person of intelligence. Tell me—by the way, I am Corono, a scientist. And you..." his hand indicated the three of them.

Larry introduced them. Corono shook his head at each name. "As I was about to say, what makes people of intelligence seek the unknown? Surely nothing but trouble is their reward, a fleeting fame, until another finds another mysterious something. But always the adventurous come rushing out to promote another bedlam. Hah! Sometimes I am sorry that the cold analytical science is my calling. But in the world of which I am a molecule, one has no choice, science or war-school. There are no others. A pity. The people of your planet who were with us for such a short time, told me a great deal of this planet you inhabit, the Earth. There were many pleasant things I heard of for the first time. A something called baseball. And another called, a burlesque show? Am I correct?"

"All the way, pal," Forgan was the one who answered. "All the way."

"STRANGE," Corono said musingly. "There was one among them who also called me pal. Yes. I am going to find many things of interest on Earth..."

"You mean you people are going to *invade* the Earth?" Larry asked.

"Dear me," Corono said, making sucking sounds with his lips. "I let the secret out. I shouldn't have, really. Excuse me, but Miss Kane has had her memory taken. And now, Mister Forgan... Fine," he went on after checking the instrument for Forgan. "I believe it is a military secret. But I *hate* secrets. I like things out in the open, friendship and enmity. Yes, your planet will be invaded. We are now in communication with the people of Venus. In fact we are expecting a number of their leaders, a sort of war council, shortly. Shouldn't wonder if no harm will come to you until the Venusians have had a chance to talk to you and the others.

"Besides, Miss Kane is the first of the opposite sex the bird-man has ever seen. She might prove of amusement to him."

"Why is the name bird-man used in the singular?" Larry asked. "There must have been a million birds in that huge aviary—at least that many."

"I thought you looked intelligent," Corono said. "But it will have to wait for a short while. Mister Forgan is through. You're next, Larry…"

Larry looked at Forgan as he stepped away from the machine and noticed that there was an odd blankness about his eyes, but did not think too much of it. Then he was seated in the same chair as the others had used and Corono was making the proper adjustments for him. Corono's voice came as from a distance, "Focus your eyes on the crosspiece…"

Larry did as the other ordered. The hairs of the crosspiece showed bright and clear against the ground glass. He looked at them as the other had told him to. Suddenly they were no longer there. Instead, a young boy and a dog walked into his vision. They were so real, so close, Larry felt he could have reached out and touched them. His lips framed the word, "Tex," but no sound came forth. He remembered exactly where Tex and he were going. To the stream on Mister Brown's place. The boy and dog faded from view. Another scene; it was a football field. A man was running with the ball. The man was without helmet, and he ran with a wondrous swaying movement of hips and body. Time after time someone attempted to stop him, but always the young man evaded the wild rushes, and out flung arms. There was a wild roaring sound. "Lipton! Run, Larry!" Then another figure came into view. That one was running parallel to the man who was carrying the football cuddled in one arm. It was Forgan, a younger, not so beat-up Forgan. Suddenly there was a someone directly in front of the ball carrier, a someone who would refuse to be drawn to either side by the swaying hips and twisting body, a someone who had never missed a tackle in all his football career. The ball carrier and tackler neared to where they were going to meet head-on. And from out of the nowhere another figure catapulted into the would-be tackler and knocked him out of the play... "Good old Focus," Larry whispered. And another scene: A long line of battlewagons. Bursts of fire broke the surface of Venus and the night was filled with roaring sounds. Then the battlewagons broke into flaming hells, and after a while the firing ceased on Venus. Below, fifty thousand feet above the cloud-filled planet, a thousand fighter ships fought singly and in groups. There was one, a single-manned ship that broke from a dogfight and chased a Venusian ship on whose side was painted the insignia of a flight commander. The two little ships spun and whirled through the screaming night until a tiny burst of green flame from the other fighter touched the side of the Venusian craft. It burst apart with a single spectacular show of flame. The man in the Earth ship grinned crookedly, and sought another victim. And the cross hairs came into view again.

"All right, Larry," Corono's voice came to him as from a distance and Larry stepped away from the machine.

He had trouble focusing properly for a few moments. Then he felt the touch of Corono's fingers and he snapped out of the daze he was in.

"All done, Earthman," Corono said. "Now we must return. Let me give you a word of warning. Do not attempt to cross the bird-man. It will not go well with you."

ONCE MORE they were in the huge aviary. Savor stood rigidly at attention as he related what the memory machine had given. The bird-man flew back and forth, back and forth, before them as Savor talked.

"Very well, Savor. You may stay without," the bird-man said. "I will call you when we have done talking."

Savor saluted and closed the huge doors behind him.

"Now I understand more clearly why the Venusians want to come to my side," the bird-man said. "They lost the war against the Earth. But they are an arrogant race, the little I have seen of them. Also a treacherous race.

"Tell me, Earthman. What do you think of my chances of having the Earth submit to me without battle?"

"Not a chance in a million," Larry said.

"I thought as much. A pity. There will be a veritable famine of living beings when I have done. I would rather not. After all, I seek only sanctuary for my people. But as is always the way, this seeking, the reasons for it, can be misconstrued. So death is done, in wholesale lots, of course. Tell me, Earthman. Do I ask too much?"

"I don't know what else you want, bird-man," Larry said boldly. "There may be hidden things, things you haven't spoken of."

The childish laughter climbed the scale until it approached the sound the mad give off. "Oh, Earthman," the bird-voice gasped. "I like you! Very much. You, at least, have intelligence. We are people who place a high value on cerebration. But we are a dying race. One that needs to plant trees that bear fruit. There is but one sex on that dead place from which we have come. The millions of years of evolution forced us in a direction that finally eliminated the other sex. So the Earth will be the fruit-bearing orchard in which I shall plant the seeds."

"Y'know what I think," Forgan said suddenly breaking in on them. "I think both of you are nuts. What goes with this deal? We're standing around shooting off our mouth to a sparrow. Why..." He suddenly reached out and grasped the bird. "Gotcha! One squeeze, you filthy thing, and..."

Suddenly Forgan stiffened. The bird-man was still clasped in the huge fingers, but laxly now. Larry had the feeling the bird could have escaped had it wanted to. But his eyes were on Forgan. He heard Gloria moan in sudden terror, and he himself felt an urge to scream. Forgan's mouth had begun to twitch, his eyes rolled, and a vibration seemed to possess the entire figure of the man. Saliva drooled from the corner of the mouth. Then the hand holding the bird-man fell limply to the side and Forgan began an odd shuffle which ended in a hopping on first one leg, then another. The arms lifted and began to flap, as if he were imitating a bird's movement before taking off.

LARRY BIT his lip until it bled. He whirled and grabbed Gloria to him, holding her head against his chest, so that she would not have to look at the horror that was taking place before them.

For Forgan was undergoing a horrible transformation.

His body was shrinking, changing. The head also was shrinking. But where the rest of the *thing* had become a bird, emerging from the garments of a man, the head had merely shrunk to a horrible miniature of itself. The mouth opened and a wild chirping came forth. Then the wings flapped and the bird, which had once been Focus Forgan, fluttered off on unsure wings to join the millions of others.

And the childish laughter of the bird-man rose until Larry wanted to hold his ears to shut out the mad sound. He didn't know how long he could have taken it. Gloria's faint pulled him back to reality and reason.

"Oh, don't worry about your friend," the bird-man said. "He will be quite content in my aviary. They all are. And when the time comes he will be released. I dislike violence, especially when it is attempted against me. Bear it in mind, Earthman. As I said before, I like you, Earthman. And the woman, also. Do not try foolish bravado, and we will get along well. Perhaps I may even take you to Venus and let you see how a planet is conquered. I—" a strange look passed over the face of the man-bird, like a cloud presaging the first of those bringing a storm, "—I think the time has come for your departure. Corono will be your guardian. He wants it, the scientific fool. Savor!"

The warrior came in and received instructions to bring the two to Corono. And once more the great doors closed behind them, Gloria was sobbing without restraint, as they followed Savor down the now-familiar corridor.

LARRY STRODE up and down the width of the

room. Corono was seated at a long couch, eating abstractedly at some fruit. Now and then Larry paused and looked out of the opening that showed the hundreds of other immense skyscrapers in the immediate vicinity. Gloria, whom Corono had given a powder, which he said would ease her mind and let her sleep, was lying in another room adjoining the one the two men were in. It was Corono's private apartment.

"Exercise of this nature leads to frustration," the scientist observed. "There is so little which you can do, you know."

"But you say, 'little,'" Larry said, stopping his wild pacing. "Which means there is a chance of doing something."

"The meaning of a word, a semantic science," Corono observed. "The way of hope. To seize on the straw and imagine it the log. Nature can suddenly erupt as it has sometimes done, for no reason we have ever been able to figure, and we will all die in the cataclysm. Of course there is hope. But hope only of Death, the final escape."

"This *thing,*" Larry grunted. "This bird-man, knows that you are against him and what he is planning. He thinks you are a fool."

Corono smiled. "It is that fact alone that might have a later meaning for us," he said. "The actions of a fool are hard to predict, simply because a fool does not work from a cerebrated pattern."

"You like that word, don't you?" Larry asked.

"I like all words. And sometimes use them in different ways. They are simply a means of communication. We use different ones for different people. The point is that we must communicate by means of the word. One way or another. Our success in having understanding can only be measured by the degree to which we have transmitted the words that can be understood."

"But the tiny beast in his large cage isn't interested in words. Deeds are his forte. Vile, vicious deeds," Larry observed.

"By the way," Corono said. "He is called, Gundar, the King... Oh, I don't say that Gundar and the military are not thinking people. I only say their pattern is not ours. For the present we are being used to make the pattern complete. I am sure Gundar will give us the same release he has given millions, and I and my friends will wind up flying about the bars of his aviary, also."

"What is this horrible power he has?" Larry asked.

For the first time the saturnine expression changed to one of deep concern and something of sadness. "I—I don't know," Corono admitted. "I don't know. Each King is given the *power,* as it is called. How it is given, how it works, is something that is a mystery to all. Aah! If only we knew. How much smoother the path would be. It is a terrible thing indeed. I have lost many friends to that power. And it is impossible to say when he will use it, when the whim will seize him."

Larry found a chair close to the couch and sat, one arm thrown over the back, his profile to Corono. "I wonder what the people back in the states are thinking?" he said. "Tom, Flynn and the others. The audience that sat up to take in the tele-cast we were supposed to do? I wonder if they have sent out search ships for us? Hah! I wonder a lot of things. Any answers to some of them, scientist?"

"Only that patience finds its own reward," the other observed. "I can tell you this. The Venusian delegation has arrived. So it shan't be long, now."

"By the way, Corono," Larry suddenly asked, turning toward the other. "How come you don't have wings as Savor and his men do?"

Corono smiled. "A matter of demand. They must use those wings. We never have reason to."

"No. No, I mean are they real?" Larry persisted.

"They are as artificial as the men using them," the other said. "Some day you will see. And like a scientist without his instruments, so is the warrior without his wings. Emptiness personified."

There was an interval of silence, an interval broken by Larry's windy sigh, and his words, "Well, I hate this doing nothing. I hope the delegation brings action."

"It will," Corono promised.

CHAPTER FOUR

HE WAS RIGHT. Since there was no means of measuring time, except by watching his watch, which was simply a waste of time, Larry had no means of knowing how long they had been in Corono's custody, before the summons came to appear before Gundar. Their stay had not been unpleasant. Food of different variety had been given them, a certain amount of freedom was theirs, and after a time he and Gloria had became somewhat accustomed to the day without end.

He had learned that the city had been constructed in an amazingly short time, and that Gundar had it in his power to construct like cities all over the Earth if he so desired. Larry also learned that the scientists of the Earth were fledglings in their knowledge alongside of Corono and his men. He had also learned Corono was the scientist supreme in all of the land, which held three other cities beside Koba.

These bits of knowledge he had gained did not sit well on his mind. Fear was a perpetual bird, sitting on his shoulder. A bird named Gundar.

He had done his best not to communicate this fear to Gloria. But she was not the sort of person to hide things from. For one thing she was too intelligent not to reason these things out for herself. And for another, she was too self-sufficient, too much a person of integrity to withhold the facts of the case. There had come a time when Larry had to tell her what he had learned from Corono and what their chances of escape were.

"Well," she had said. "If there is even the smallest chance we must not give up hope. In the meantime, we must try to figure out a means of getting back to Earth, so that should the chance present itself we would be prepared."

Then came the summons. And once more Savor appeared before them. There was a look of triumph on the warrior's face. And for once Corono had no wit to throw off at the other. It was all-too apparent that Savor and his warriors were to see action. But for the first time he did not act with the complete disregard of the Earth people as he had before. It did not mean that he himself had changed. But the fact that Gundar had allowed them to live was warrant enough that they must be treated as humans. At least of Koba's status.

There were some fifty of the Venusians, huge men,

most of them well over seven feet in height, their skins a slate grey, their eyes yellow as a jungle cat's. They wore the trappings of the warrior caste, and the belts that held their energy pistols were studded with precious stones. It was the outward sign of their overweening vanity— that and their nose-high disdain of anything that could not battle. Fighting was their life and to it they dedicated their living.

As usual Gundar flew back and forth among them, and between them. It was hard to say whether they feared the bird-man or not. But that they held him in respect was easily to be seen. At sight of the two Earth people Gundar flew to meet them. He hovered at eye level and called their names as if in introduction. There were several names familiar to Larry, names well known in inter-planetary circles.

ONE, SAX-O, was well known for his space travels. Another, Gin-Per, had invented a gravity-deflector that proved invaluable when meeting the huge asteroids of space. But the one that elicited the most surprise was Hag-U, the commander-in-chief of all the forces that had been defeated in the war between the Earth and Venus.

Larry wondered how he got here. He had been banished forever, to spend the last of his days on one of the satellites of Saturn.

"If you are worried for your friend," Gundar said, "do not feel too concerned. He is quite content."

It was strange, Larry thought, that just the slightest thought of Forgan had come to his mind, a thought that had been brought up only as they entered the huge aviary and he had looked up at the bars holding the myriad birds. But it brought back to mind what the friendly soldier had once told him. About the reading of minds.

"I hope so," Larry said. "He is a friend, and I do worry."

The evil face, tiny as a miniature, grinned at the answer. "Always from the emotional standpoint, eh, Earthman. Cold reason serves us better. Much better. No interference. But the council is ready. There are seats, my friends…"

For a moment after they were seated there was the hoarse sound of many voices in low talk. Then Gundar flew to a bar suspended just a few feet above the floor level. He perched upon it and swayed gently to and fro, the while he surveyed his audience.

"My friends," he began. "I have called us together because the time has come for, on the one hand, vengeance, and on the other, sanctuary. I speak for all of the dead planet of Cycle Three. And you are the representatives of the planet, Venus.

"I have also asked two people who are here visiting, as it were, from the planet, Earth, to attend. Since it is their planet that will be the scene of our conquest it is only proper they should know of and about it, and the means to be used in its accomplishment."

Laughter roared out at the words. And it was instantly noticeable that the Venusians became more at ease. This creature, this bird-man, was to their liking. For after all, weren't they the cruelest people in the Universe?

Gundar went on: "We have struck a pact, my people

and the people of Venus. In return for our scientific knowledge and machines, we will have the planet Venus for our sanctuary, while the people of Venus take Earth."

Loud cheers roared out at the words.

Larry was aghast. So that was their diabolic scheme. What a horror was to be loosed on the Earth!

"So was the pact made and will be kept," Gundar went on. "My warriors are few and those of Venus many. Enough so that they will overrun Earth.

"And now I tell you that it will soon take place. Very soon. My scientists have told me all is in readiness. The vessels that we used in our migration to this place are ready for the larger travel, the more dangerous journey. But first the way must be made safe. I am prepared to send the machines and science weapons. Are you ready to use them?"

A concerted roar of "Ayes" rose up to greet the bird-man's shouted question.

"Good! Then within a very short time we will go to work. Now I am tired and must ask you to leave me. There are quarters prepared for your comfort for the time you will be here. The moment of departure will be made known to you…"

Larry arose with the Venusians, and Gloria started to follow suit. But both paused as Gundar said:

"Hold, Earthmen. I would speak with you."

HE WAITED until the last of the Venusians departed before speaking again:

"You will return to Corono's apartment. I have decided that since you have found favor in his eyes, you will both travel in his private spaceship. It will be a vantage point for you to watch the spectacle of the destruction of the cities of Earth.

"As for your friend, who is in my aviary somewhere, he also will be with you. In a cage, of course. Do not despair. It is entirely within the bounds of reason that I will find use for both of you. The woman intrigues me. I have never before met anyone of her sex. Yes. I think I will find use for you. When next we meet it will be on Earth…"

Corono's smile of welcome was heartfelt, and Larry felt that it was like seeing a dear friend after a long and frightening journey. Both men clothed their real feelings in their own fashion.

Corono said, as they stepped into the now-familiar apartment: "No wings? I *am* surprised! Gundar loves to make his power felt. And it is easy to displease him. I heard of a man who once breathed too heavily. Gundar thought the proper cure for that was to make him a winged creature."

Gloria had pleaded a headache and had gone immediately into the room she had occupied. Larry was alone with the scientist. He grinned broadly at the other and replied:

"A sort of asthmatic bird, eh?" he turned serious. "It won't be long, now, Corono. This, from Gundar's crooked, evil mouth. The Venusians almost broke the doors down with their noise. They *are* a noisy race. And their wars are conducted loudly also. It's as if they have fear in their souls and without sound to reassure them they are lost. We learned that in the war and capitalized on it. All our attacks were made in the utmost secrecy and with the most astonishing quiet.

"You told me that you have created machines the like of which have never been seen or thought of. I can well believe it, having lived here in Koba. We have cities that are similar. But only to the casual eye. Just a few items. 'The flying bridges', a thousand feet high, thin as a spider's cobweb, strong as the strongest Solminum. And these glassless windows. I don't quite understand them. Nothing lies between us and the air out there. Yet if I try to put my hand out beyond the frame I find it impossible.

"But we also are clever. I am sure it will be a long and costly affair."

"My friend," Corono began on a note of sadness. "And I do consider you a friend. For surely I have learned to love and respect you, as man does a friend. My friend, let me make several things clear to you, that you do not lift your hopes too high. Gundar is evil incarnate. We are not possessed of morals, nor do we have concepts of right and wrong, such as, for example, you have. Our's has been a far more complex way of life than yours. So, early, we learned in our evolution that the fewer the interferences from the hazards of these things, the better are our lives. They were tossed aside as having no value. Because we are neuters, sexless, we have no love, as you know it. Emotion is something strange to us. Neither love nor hate. We have, in fact, become neuters in the strict sense of the word.

"But this I say, as a man and a scientist. It is wrong. In my heart I have always said it. Now the words are spoken. But I am a small part of my world and, truth to tell, a very unimportant part. Gundar uses me as he does the seeds with which he is fed. When he has taken the kernel from it he spits it out. So will I be rejected when the times comes."

"Look," Larry said after a while. Corono had fallen into a dark and introspective silence. "I'd never asked before, it never occurred to me. Now I'd like to know. What is Gundar? How was he made? What is this terrible power he has over all of you? Why do you all fear him? And why does he stay in that monstrous cage, closed in with all those birds?"

"Many questions, and all answered with a single answer," Corono said. "Gundar is the spirit of evil. Strange. We are supposed not to have concepts of good and evil, yet I use the word and have knowledge of its connotation. I must think on it. Perhaps I have opened up a new field of speculation..."

LARRY BROKE in. He knew Corono could go on for hours once a thought had come to him on which he could build. Larry wanted to know these things. "Later, Corono. About Gundar—"

"...Yes, Gundar. I don't know whether I can make it clear to you. Suppose I say that he is the father of us all. Would you understand more clearly? No, I don't think you would. Or should I say that our evolution began with a bird instead of a monkey. But you couldn't understand that either."

"Hold it!" Larry cried. "How did you know we began with an anthropoid? I never mentioned evolution to you."

"It was just in your mind," Corono smiled as gave answer. "I know this business of telepathy bothers you.

It does me, sometimes, too. For the same reason. I don't understand it either. But every now and then we can 'read' someone's mind. Gundar can do it all the time. So let's get back to the birds.

"Gundar is actually the father of us all; he was the past, is the present and will be the future: He is eternal. You don't believe it, do you?"

He had seen the shocked look in Larry's eyes.

"Are you trying to say Gundar is…" He didn't want to continue. It would be sacrilege.

"Whatever you wish to call him," Corono replied. "The race of evolution is about over. We have developed to the point where there is nothing in the beyond. So up there on Cycle Three we were faced with extinction because our creation and continuance was not a matter of race continuance by natural means.

"So some time in the past Gundar created men. Yes, Larry, I am a mutation. But not as you think of such, not a robot, an emptiness of mind, of spirit. Perhaps Gundar did not think we would be as we are. He created us to his immediate needs, the warrior and the man of science. We are the thinking kind, the warrior the acting. There are a hundred of us, altogether. The men you saw in the laboratory."

"But if Gundar is all," Larry said in shrewd observation, "he is also the motivation and the spirit. The two of you are synonymous, surely."

"I sometimes wonder," Corono said. "Nor do I ever believe it will be made known to me."

ONCE MORE silence fell between them. Each wrapped the cloak of his thoughts about himself, each lost in memory.

"And the many birds…?" Larry asked in a low voice. "What meaning have they?"

"They are the dead," Corono said. "The dead in life."

"So Forgan is dead," Larry said softly. "I—I'm sorry to hear it. He was a roughneck, a loudmouthed character. Yet I knew him well, and I suppose loved him. For he was part of me, although he said he hated me, a part of me that was like an arm or leg."

"No," came the startling words from Corono. "Forgan is *not* dead. He is still alive. Just a bird, that is all. Did you ever notice that only Gundar flutters down from his perch. The others never do, I believe that their incessant chatter is but the cries of anger against Gundar. Someday, maybe, some of those birds will escape. I don't know what will happen when they do. Nor have I any idea. But it would be interesting to see. And be there."

A chime struck somewhere and a light flashed in a far corner. The time had come for food. Corono had explained it to Larry. Since there were but two classes of men, warriors and scientists, the scientists had had to invent a means of preparing and servicing the distribution of food. It was one of the marvels Larry wished they had on Earth. Everything worked on a time schedule. There were huge kitchens that ran themselves. Food was grown artificially, prepared and sent to all parts of Koba by means of a conveyer belt system.

Corono stepped to the wall section that held the food opening, slid the door aside and lifted out the tray and carried it to the couch. "Would you call Miss Kane, Larry?" he said.

Sleep had done her good, Gloria realized, as she answered to Larry's knock. He stood in the doorway, staring down at her. He *was* handsome. And these weeks? months? years? Or maybe minutes? had made a change in her mind about him.

She had not liked him when they first met. At Rainier he had been pleasant, but patronizingly so, she thought. But under the stress of danger he had shown a side she had not known of. First it had been admiration. Then as time went by the admiration deepened into something stronger. She was not yet ready to admit that love had come into her life.

"Hi, Larry," she greeted him, stretching and rubbing at her eyes with gently pressing fingertips.

"Greetings, Gloria," he said. "Have a nice sleep? I won't even ask about your headache. Corono's pills do wonders."

"Yes, they do." Her lovely eyes clouded. "If only they could make me forget that, that—" she hesitated, hating to even mention Gundar's name or shape. "Oh, well. Let's eat. There's a heck of a variety. I'm always excited by lunch or dinner or breakfast."

Larry laughed aloud. It felt good to laugh. She was right, though. The stuff looked appetizing, smelled good, but had no taste whatsoever.

SHE MOVED past him, her body filled with rhythm, her shoulders straight and her head high. She tossed him a wink over her shoulder and he winked in reply. *She* would never let him down.

They were washing the meal down with the red liquid Larry called Chianti, when the summons came. They were to be ready on the instant. The invasion of Earth was to take place...

The sky was filled with spaceships. They were of all shapes and sizes, from the trim, teardrop fighters, to the huge sky freighters, each carrying a hundred thousand fighting men. The silver shape of Venus was fading from view.

The wide pilot's seat held three. Corono's plane was a sleek job of his own design. As fast as the swiftest fighter, it had no armament. But as Corono said, "We are safe. Nothing can touch us. I have seen to it. And if there is a fight it will be proved. Like it, Larry?"

But there was no need for the Earthman to answer. He had been filled with admiration from the instant he had stepped into the small cabin compartment. He looked at the instrument panel. How simple. No great show of glass faces with mysterious dials, such as the ships he was used to. Here there were three dials, mysterious only in that, instead of numbers, there were characters. A stick did the maneuvering, just like in the planes of the twentieth century. There was nothing else.

"I sure do." Larry was emphatic. He looked over his shoulder at the birdcage swinging gently to and fro with each movement of the ship. "How about you, Focus?"

"Ah, man," said Forgan. "What a sweet job. Too bad we can't have a tele-cast of what's going to be. And I just wish that guy Gundar would only have let me change back to the way I was."

Larry shook his head in wonder. An orderly had walked up, carrying a covered cage, just as they were about to take off. Within the cage was Forgan. And Forgan spoke English, not the bird chatter they had expected. His wizened face, smaller than a monkey's, resembled one in miniature. But the features were the same, as were his caustic comments on Gundar and what he wished he could do. They had asked him if he had a memory of what took place while he was in the aviary, but he didn't. Memory had returned of a sudden. Darkness enfolded him. Then light appeared and with it the faces of Gloria, Larry and Corono.

THEY HAD placed him on a perch designed for his use. Now he was a member of their crew, useless except for his talk that always had the faculty of stimulating Larry if only toward mayhem.

"Too bad fly-boy couldn't have had this job to play with. Wouldn't he be a hero to the gals back in the states. How about that, handsome?"

"Y'know, Forgan," Larry said, turning back to looking through the wide opening that showed a view of all the Heavens, "some day I'm going to clip those wings. Then you'll be like the fly in the molasses. You won't like that."

"There'll never be the day you could lick me, one way or another. Even as a bird, I can still take you. Wanna try?"

"No. I'll wait for the day your ugly self will be back to normal. Then we'll settle what we started a couple of times."

"And when that time comes," Forgan replied, "I'll take you like I always have."

Corono was always amused by their exchanges. It was a stimulating talk. Nothing intellectual, yet it showed a depth of feeling foreign to him. He liked it. "I hope the time comes," Corono said. "I would like to see what happens. Forgan has the strength. But I think Larry has the skill."

"Ain't never been a boxer could take a puncher," Forgan said. "I'll knock him right out of his shoes."

"I think," said a soft voice, "that we are going to have some excitement soon."

But they had already seen what Gloria noticed. The fighters, whole clouds of them, were peeling off into formations. It was the signal of approaching enemy craft. The sound of a buzzer was heard to break the silence and Corono fiddled with a small dial close to his right hand. Strange sounds filled the cabin, sounds that made sense to Corono but none to the others. And after a moment the sounds ceased.

"They have sighted the first attackers," Corono said. "We have orders to stay away from the fighting. So we'll have a box seat, as Mister Forgan calls it."

The ships of the Venusian fleet were easy to distinguish. Larry, Forgan and the girl were familiar with their markings. But for a while they had found it difficult to tell what shapes the ships of Gundar's fleet were. They took the shapes of clouds, of meteor tails, of tiny asteroids, of all the natural phenomena of the heavens.

Then the first of the Earth's fleet hove into view. The breaths of the three Earth people quickened at sight of the huge superdreadnoughts, the slick fighters, the tenders, slow and cumbrous, feeding energy to the large vessels. Larry knew what the scene would be on one of those immense creations.

Men would be at battle stations. Everything would be

secure. Hundreds of thousands of men, equipped with space suits, would be in readiness for boarding orders, their heat rifles and pistols at hand. In the meantime the tiny fighters, like hundreds of thousands of raindrops, would dart here and there among the enemy, dealing a quick blow at the belly of this freighter, engaging the enemy in dog fights, their green flames shooting from the gun mounts, as if St Elmo's fire had enveloped them.

"Watch," Corono's voice came as from a distance to Larry.

Larry's eyes followed the line of the scientist's pointing finger. A long line of troop carriers stretched in an immense arc across the heavens. They were protected by a veritable swarm of fighters and cruisers. The fighters and cruisers shot out to meet the Earth ships. And again Corono said, "Watch."

SUDDENLY, from both sides of the large ships, streams of flame poured. Larry had never seen anything like it. The flame was a separate entity. It left the muzzles of the guns and shot out for thousands of miles. And joined with the flames of all the ships. In an incredibly short time the entire troop-carrying contingent was surrounded, as it were, by an immense halo of living flame that moved with the vessels at the same rate of speed.

In the meantime several of the fighters had broken through the circle of protectors. Straight for the troop ships they dove. And as they met the line of flame a terrible thing happened. The tiny craft simply disintegrated.

A horrified sound came from Gloria. But Larry could

only curse under his breath. "Get those blasted devils!" Forgan yelled. But Larry knew it was in vain.

Another large group of fighters rushed to break through. And with them were the cruisers, heavier-armored, carrying stronger, more powerful guns. And as with the first, so with these. They vanished leaving not even a trace behind them.

"Well," Larry sighed. "Guess the troop ships are safe enough. Until they try to land. There are anti-special guns that could wreck them."

"All taken into consideration," Corono said. "Watch what happens to your dreadnoughts."

It was a terrible thing to watch, the disintegration of a proud and once-mighty fleet. Especially to men who were once part of it. But after the first single battles it became evident that the Earth ships could match the others in no way except speed. Retreat sounded for the remnants and they fled Earthward singly and in groups.

"All over now but the landing," Corono said.

CHAPTER FIVE

BUT HE was wrong.

It proved to be a little tougher than he had thought it would be. Many strange and powerful weapons had been added to the armament of the Earth's forces since Larry was a member of the air force. The scientific knowledge of all the nations of the Earth had been pooled. Though Gundar did not know it the Earth had spies in the various Venusian courts. And since the Venusians could no more talk with braggadocio, it was only inevitable that the Earth would learn of the invasion. It was simply a matter of how much time would be permitted the defenders.

The first the invaders knew of it was when the bombers received orders to come in on their runs. Not a single Earth ship opposed them as they shot down to about ten thousand miles of the Earth and started on their runs. They started on their runs and completed them. But something was obviously wrong. There should have been some visible signs of bombing in the screen that showed the area on Earth to be bombed. It was the vast New York section, six hundred square miles. Yet Larry and the others saw the skyscrapers still standing.

A mellow glow suddenly came to life in the cabin and directly above their heads the face of a man showed first then, in a second or two, the entire figure. It was Gundar. But a Gundar they had never seen before. This was a young man, tall and handsome, wearing the uniform of his rank, of which there was but one. A circlet of some strange glowing metal held silver hair in place. A pair of huge wings sprouted from his shoulder blades. But though it was a younger, more handsome Gundar, the evil in his face and eyes was no less than when he had the shape of the tiny bird.

"The Earth people," Gundar's younger, more mellowed voice began, "have proved they are no mean opponents. Therefore plan X will have to be followed until we have had a chance to study this new development. Corono! It is your duty to break through this veil of force they have thrown up against bombardment."

As quickly as it had appeared so did the light die. The

three in the seat looked at one another. Corono's face showed the strain he was under. There was no choice. And he knew that it was only a matter of mental arithmetic before the formula of force would be worked out. It would be the end then.

"Corono," Larry's voice broke in on his reverie.

"Yes?"

"You once said you were the greatest scientist in Cycle Three. Are there any your equal?"

"I don't understand," Corono said.

"If you don't solve the puzzle, can anyone else?" Larry persisted.

Gloria and Forgan knew what he was driving at. The bird and the girl held their breaths. On Corono's answer might hinge the fate of the Earth.

"Perhaps," Corono said. "I'm not sure. There are some who might after a lengthy period. I can. In a very short time."

Larry bent his head as if in prayer. "Well Corono," he said. "We have become friends, haven't we? You hate Gundar. I have seen it time after time. Hate and fear him. But remember this. He can make you die but once. Refuse him. Call him and say you won't do it."

"I can't," Corono said. And suddenly winked broadly. "On the other hand surely it won't be my fault if you take over this ship by overpowering me. After all I am a scientist, not a warrior. It would not be expected of me to risk my life…"

Gloria leaned forward and planted a kiss squarely on his mouth. His sallow features crimsoned. "I—I'm not sure," Corono said. "But I think I liked it."

LARRY looked at his watch that he had never forgotten to wind, meaningless as it had been. Four minutes had gone by since Gundar had appeared in the overhead screen. He sighed softly and said in low tones:

"Just turn sideways, pal. It won't hurt too much."

Corono did as he was bid. The uppercut that knocked him out was delivered with the same exactness and precision as a surgeon's scalpel making an incision. Corono slumped to one side. And Larry took the controls.

He had timed it to the second. Once more the mellow light appeared and after the face and figure of Gundar.

"What is wrong, Corono?" Gundar demanded. Then his eyes narrowed, as if he were looking straight into their cabin. "I see," he said softly. "Well, I have no time to waste…" the light did not fade as Gundar's voice did. It simply went out, as the old-fashioned electric bulb. And as it went out, the tiny vessel lurched and slipped. Larry twisted at the control stick. It moved as his fingers directed, but loosely, without bearing.

"Damn," Larry said softly. "We're out of control."

"So bring the guy out of it," Forgan suggested in his bird-voice.

"Of course," Gloria said.

"I guess I'm scared. Gundar isn't fooled easily."

"So it'll be one way or another," Forgan said.

Larry took Corono's head between his palms and shook him gently back and forth, massaging the nerves of the neck, stimulating the muscles. He could feel a pulse in the man's neck pounding steadily and surely. And after a while Corono's eyes fluttered, then opened wide. A silly grin parted his lips.

"Wha-what happened?" he asked.

"I knocked you out," Larry said.

"You did? And not a blow struck in my own defense. They'll call me coward," Corono said smiling broadly.

"They'll call you but you won't hear if you don't do something about this crate," Forgan said. "We're out of control."

"What?" Corono sat straight up at the words. "But that's impossible. We can't be."

"Then you take over," Larry said. "I can't make anything work."

The saturnine look returned to Corono's face again as he played with the controls. "I always maintained Gundar was the greatest scientist of us all. Imagine. By will alone he has thrown us out of control. Incredible."

"Never mind the compliments," Forgan's oddly raucous voice demanded. "Can you get us in control?"

"Yes. But Gundar must take his mind from us. The instant he does I will take over. Or rather Larry will. He is a pilot. And it will be up to him to make the ship behave as if it were still out of control. Gundar will have to think of something else. Especially if they have not solved the mystery of the block the Earth people have thrown up."

THEY WERE within the Earth's gravity. Their fall was directly into the Earth. Moments of vast tension went by. Drops of sweat appeared on Larry's brow as the minutes ticked by, Corono's face assumed a look of intense absorption. His knuckles held so tight to the control stick they became white from the pressure.

"Aah," a windy sigh dropped from Corono's lips.

"Take over, Larry. We're in control again."

Larry slid into the seat occupied by the other. Corono had not given him an easy task. The ship had to lurch and act crazily, just as a ship would that had gone out of control. Further, they might fall into the path of an Earth fighter ship as they neared the planet. Sweat poured from his face as he concentrated in getting free of all the obstacles.

He could not tell how many hundreds of thousands of miles they fell. He knew without looking that they had left the invading fleet far behind. But the one worry he had was getting safely to Earth.

"A million miles," Corono said. "Soon we will accelerate. By the time we have fallen another half million miles I will have figured out a way to get past the force blockade. I am sure it is that. Just keep control…"

But two thirds of the distance passed before Corono had it figured.

"There are weak spots in the force blanket," he said. "When we pass a certain point I will let you know. You will dive straight at the figure I show you on this dial. Keep it constant. Once we are within the Earth's atmosphere it will have to be up to your expert piloting to get us away from any fighter craft."

Time passed quickly. Then came the command. "Now!"

Larry depressed the stick and the ship responded on the instant. Their belts held them snugly and the cage in which Forgan was enclosed stood almost level. But there was no increase in pressure and after a while they became used to the terrific speed.

As a shaft of sunlight breaking through a cloud blanket so did they break into the Earth's atmosphere. Corono leaned forward and twisted at the second of the three dials. Their speed lessened immediately.

"Too fast to land at that rate," he said. "The rest is up to you. Just nod your head when you want to come in and I'll set it at landing speed."

Larry kept a sharp eye peeled for fighter craft. They were at the level he expected to find them. But not a thing was to be seen. Then they were at the cloud level of thirty thousand feet and Larry nodded. Below, they could see a green land. To the right lay a small range of mountains or high hills. Then as they swept lower they saw the shores of a wide ocean. Corono's eyes went wide. He had never seen the likes of it.

"The Pacific, I think," Larry said. "Well. Here we come in."

They landed without a jar. Corono pressed a small lever and the hatch opened. In a moment the three, Larry holding the cage with Forgan, stepped to the ground.

"Let me out," Forgan said. "The good old U. S. A. I want to kiss it."

"I feel the same way. But we don't have time. We've got to get to the authorities."

"Yes," said Corono. "And we'd better hurry. There won't be too much time."

It proved to be the most amazing thing but they had landed within fifty miles of the spot from which the momentous flight had begun. A farmer picked the three up and drove them into the nearest town, a suburb of Los Angeles.

It had been spring, the first part of May, when they had left. Now it was early summer. They could see the signs of it on all hands as they drove along the mountain road. Somehow they felt no surprise. But they did feel actual shock when they arrived within the environs of Los Angeles proper.

The farmer, a quiet man with steady eyes under thick brows, did not ask many questions. But his answers were direct and to the point, when they asked what had happened since their departure. Of course he did not see Forgan. Larry had thrown his kerchief over the small cage.

It seemed the Earth had known of the impending invasion for a month and had feverishly prepared for it. Los Angeles was deserted of civilian population. There were a hundred camps all along the mountain stretch from L. A. all the way to San Francisco. The military alone were permitted within the city limits.

It was to headquarters that Larry asked to be delivered. But the farmer could only take them to the first outpost.

A lieutenant took them in tow and shortly after they arrived at a garrison point. Here a colonel interviewed them. And saw to it they received a pass to proceed directly to the headquarters of General James McCall, chief of command in the Los Angeles area.

General McCall, a tall man with stern features, dressed in the quiet greys of a command officer, stood at their entrance. He offered his hand to Larry and Corono and bowed to the girl.

"I have been notified of your safe landing, and congratulate you both. But at the moment I am not in a position to provide the necessary plane escort. I hope you understand…?"

Larry looked at the man with a sinking sensation at the pit of his stomach. This man wasn't like some of the military he had known, obsessed with their invulnerability and importance and not caring to hear anything that they did not understand.

"But General," he began.

"Sorry, Lipton," the General said decisively. "I haven't the time or patience to explain that we are at war with an unknown enemy. If men like you had been here at the time when the call came, instead of seeking your glory at more favorable pursuits…"

"The cage," Corono whispered. "Unveil it."

LARRY THREW the kerchief from the bars and revealed Forgan. For a second or two the General did not notice it. Then his eyes moved toward it and widened. And the words stopped dripping from his lips.

"We have just landed, General, after having escaped the enemy forces," Larry said quickly. "This is Corono, their number one scientist. We must get to Washington immediately."

"What—what is that horrible thing?" McCall asked.

"What was once a man," Larry said.

"And what's *still* a man," Forgan growled.

The General stepped back a pace at the words that came from the gargoylish thing. He looked as if he had been hearing things. And being afraid to believe them.

"If we delay much longer it may be too late," Corono's smooth voice urged. "Gundar can finish it all very quickly, once he lands. He will use the bird-warriors as a spearhead for the Venusian hordes."

Perhaps it was the mention of the Venusians? Perhaps it had been the sight of Forgan? But McCall suddenly swooped down on the hand mike and spoke into it. In a moment an officer in the uniform of air intelligence appeared.

"Take these people to Washington and bring them to the chief-of-staff. Give them clearance above anyone and everyone. This is triple-must important, Captain."

"This way, folks," the Captain said, ushering them from the General's presence.

It was hard to say which felt the better for the departure, the General or the four who left...

THEY NEVER reached Washington. There was no Washington to get to. Nor a New York. Gundar had found a way to break through the force umbrella. Someone else had figured out that there had to be slits in it to allow ships to pass through. As Corono said, it was only a matter of mathematics...

In fact they were lucky they had the chance to land.

For suddenly, as if from nowhere, there appeared a veritable swarm of fighter craft. Corono had spotted them first.

"Gundar! He has broken through!"

"Get it down before they spot us!" Larry shouted.

Something in their tones made the Captain act on the instant. And not a second too soon. They came in at too great a speed and almost cracked up. But the Captain was an excellent pilot. They watched the enemy disappear in the direction of Los Angeles in wordless apprehension.

"Where are we, Captain?" Gloria said, breaking the silence.

"Nebraska. Maybe fifty miles from Omaha."

The sun was sinking, night was about to fall. Larry thought fast. If Gundar had indeed broken through in force, and the invasion of the Earth was on, then the safest place would be some farmhouse. The large cities would be the first to feel the brunt of the attack. It would be a while before the routing out of the last defenders was affected. Gundar had the advantage in superior space weapons but invasions were fought with men…

The Captain's name was Oglesby. He listened in stony silence to Larry's espousal of his argument, that their safety and eventual escape lay in concealment for the present. It was obvious he didn't like it.

"…But why, Captain?" Corono asked.

"Might as well fight until we can't fight any more."

"That's no answer," Larry said. "It sounds like defeatism. Might as well put the pistol to your mouth and blow out your brains right now, if you feel it's only a matter of time. It'll be a lot quicker and probably less painful."

Oglesby became angry and wanted to fight. Forgan was all for it. But Corono threw oil on the tempestuous waters. "Now hold on. Since it has become impossible to reach our goal and since there is a difference of opinion on procedure, why not let each to his own devices. Captain Oglesby, since it's your desire to get to a fighting front as quickly as possible, the ship is still in the meadow…"

Oglesby stalked off in cold fury, his bearing stiff as a

ramrod.

They watched him go with mixed emotions. "The jerk," Forgan said as the ship rose straight up and streaked off to the east.

"No," Corono said. "He isn't that. Fool, yes, but remember—he is following a set of convictions that he believes are his own."

"Aah! Nuts to him," Forgan said sourly. "What about us?"

"Well, Corono," Larry turned to the one man who might have the answer to their future, "suppose you say. What about us?"

"We will have to establish some sort of headquarters. I can give your scientists the formulas and know-how to make weapons that would enable them to fight successfully against Gundar. But this matter takes a certain amount of planning and work, and, as important, men and materials."

"Well," Larry said reflectively. "I imagine their plan of attack would be something like this. The large cities of the Earth, first. Then beachheads into the urban areas. It would take ten million men to overrun the United States alone. So they won't bother with the farm population except to establish garrisons at strategic points. Does that sound reasonable?"

Gloria shook her head in agreement and Corono nodded as if satisfied with Larry's reasoning. As usual Forgan voiced a raucous comment:

"I don't care what happens. But let me see action…"

CHAPTER SIX

CORINTHIS, Nebraska was a garrison town. Four hundred Venusians were stationed there. It was a jet-freight terminal for the wheat shipments of Kansas and Nebraska, so held a certain importance to the conquering forces of Gundar, who had proclaimed himself ruler of the planet Earth.

Night had fallen over the silent city. Not a single light showed. It was cloudy night, the moon peering fretfully from behind its curtain every now and then. When the moon showed its face the wide ribbon of concrete showed white against the dun-colored ground. And had one been a close observer one would have seen twin columns of men crawling along the grass and ditches to either side of the road.

At the head of one column Larry Lipton sneaked along on his belly. Corono matched him on the opposite side of the road. Behind them, in double rows, were two hundred men, each equipped with pistols that Corono had devised and had been made up in hand forges in a dozen farm barns along the Nebraska and Kansas borders.

Four miles to their rear, hidden well in a shallow forest, lay a number of strange looking cars, each equipped to hold twenty men and their arms. These cars looked like long grey cigars.

Larry lifted a circular disk to his lips and whispered

into it:

"Corono. We are a half-mile from the first roadblock. Disperse your men according to plan."

He counted off twenty-five seconds, then turned and whispered a command to his second in command. The shadows spread in a long thin line for a hundred yards. And Larry came to a crouching position and waved his men forward.

The Venusian roadblock consisted of twenty guards and a stone guardhouse. It was there so that all trucks bearing food shipments to Corinthis could be checked. Eight guards patrolled the road, their slate-grey bodies like tall shadows in the fitful light. When the moonlight struck them, bright bits of glittering lights cascaded from the jeweled ornaments at their waists.

The eight Venusians standing guard disappeared in thin wisps of vapor as men rose from the deep grass alongside the road and pressed the buttons at the sides of the pistols they carried. There was neither sound nor smoke nor light. Just a finger pressing at a button, and the pistol aimed correctly. Nor did it take any longer for death to come to the other twelve.

This was the first victory over Gundar in three months.

A HUNDRED miles to the east lay the town of Koropolis. It was a headquarters town for the top half of what Gundar called the third area. Six thousand Venusians were stationed here. On the same night the roadblock at Corinthis was taken, four hundred men and women in various disguises, mostly as farmers and their wives, came to the city. They came in trucks and some in old-fashioned twentieth-century farm wagons. Some came on foot. And others on the trains that Gundar allowed to come into the city twice a day.

Gundar had proclaimed the law of the conquerors— that everything is made for the use of the invaders, and for their relaxation. Koropolis was a town in normal times of fifty thousand people. With its added importance as a headquarters, it grew to triple its size. And with the coming of the Venusians, there also came the men who fattened on the misery of others, the worse-than-traitors who lived on the fats thrown off by the men who won the war. These set up shops that catered to the appetites of the Venusians.

Koropolis had become a city of inns and bawdyhouses.

And of all the inns, three became a sort of center of attraction, for both Koropolisians and Venusians. It was to these three inns that the four hundred men and women came.

A tall slender woman, whose hair was tawny and whose body was shown to effect in a tight-fitting overalled outfit affected by the wives of farmers, stepped into the huge place that was the Inn of the Clouds. Hundreds of Venusian soldiers were noisily drinking and carousing. Brooding farmers and their wives sat at many small tables along the walls. Some looked with disapproval at the number of girls who had suddenly found the company of the Venusian soldiery acceptable.

The tawny-haired woman stood at the entrance for a long moment until she felt that the eyes she wished to see had done so, then strolled with a hip-swaying movement toward a table among several others on a small platform.

Gloria Kane had spotted the insignia of the high commander of the headquarters area on the belt of one of the grey giants.

A grey giant came running forward and grabbed Gloria about the middle, his face lax, his mouth adrool from the effects of the heady liquor. His greenish eyes were aflame with desire. He crushed the girl close to him and tried to bend her back to kiss her. Suddenly he stiffened as she brought her knee up hard into his groin. Like an eel the girl slipped from his grasp and dashed across the room, a wild gleam of anger in his eyes, and a grin of derision on her lips. The giant recovered and dashed after her.

Straight to the table of the commander-in-chief Gloria ran. The giant caught her on the second of the three steps to the platform. And as his arm encircled her waist to drag her back, she looked straight into the green eyes of the stiff-backed man at the head of the table. It was as if she had thrown a spark at him. He blinked and said:

"Leave her."

For an instant the arm about her middle tightened. Then it relaxed and fell away. She didn't bother to turn to see what happened to, the man. Right up to the table she marched and seated herself on the lap of the commander. Her hand went about his neck and the fingers of the other hand caressed the large, round bald head.

"These cattle are making this place impossible," one of the officers said. "More and more are coming here. Tonight, the place is crawling with them."

"YES," ANOTHER said. "This stuff we are drinking *is* strong. Boon-da is already drunk. Does he not see that for everyone who comes in, four go out."

It was so. As if their disgust had become too great to bear, a large number of the men and women at the small wall tables had left. But their places were taken by others.

"You are charming, my dear," the commander whispered as his hand caressed her slender arm. "Very."

"And you are a hero," she replied. They did not notice that her eyes were intent on the doorway. A small smile suddenly broke on her lips.

Three men or figures of men had suddenly appeared in the doorway. The figures, dressed completely from head to toe in a sort of dun-colored outfit, blocked the entrance completely. Their hands were held low against their hips and their fingers held a small pistol. Slowly the noise and drinking stopped as more and more of the Venusians saw the strange figures.

And finally complete silence fell away.

"What is this?" the commander shouted, as he started to shove at Gloria to get her off his lap.

"Friends of mine, commander," she said, as her fingers touched the back of his neck. The wires that led down to the index finger and thumb made contact against the flesh.

The commander toppled forward on his face. It was the signal they had been waiting.

As if by magic pistols like those the three held appeared in the hands of every man and woman in the place. The Venusians died as vermin do when crushed by a stone. Faint wisps of vapor marked their passing. And the few who tried to break through the three men at the door simply disappeared as the rest.

It was a regulation that only officers could wear arms in any of the eating or drinking places. That was why Gloria had taken it on herself to sit with the officers. The instant the commander fell forward she whipped a small pistol from a hidden pocket and pressed at the button and whipped it back and forth for a couple of seconds. As if by magic the table was cleared of Venusians.

The whole thing lasted some two minutes...

And as if nothing had happened the men and women who remained took up their possessions and left. It was as if a plague had suddenly come up and taken off every living being.

That scene was repeated in the other two inns. Twelve hundred Venusians died that night. And not a soul understood how it had happened. For as simply as the four hundred men and women made their way into Koropolis, so did they make their way out.

Nor was there a single person among these four hundred missing...

GUNDAR called it 'The Room of the King.' Three hundred thousand humans had built it for him, this palace of marble and steel overlooking the wide Pacific. For some reason known only to him Gundar had liked the site though he had seen many all over the Earth. He sat and brooded, one palm holding up his chin, the fingers of the other hand lax on the arm of the chair that was an immense throne. Women of all the races and countries of the Earth, dressed in the flimsiest costumes, lolled on cushion along the walls of the gigantic room. Earthmen, traitors who had sold out to Gundar, Venusian warriors in all their trappings, and Gundar's own bird-men, stood, sat, leaned in groups, or by the side of the courtesans. Only Gundar seemed to show no interest in these women.

He had thought the entire Earth had been conquered. Commander after commander had reported this country taken and that until at the end there was nothing left to conquer. Then had come the first disquieting news. A small garrison in a Nebraska town had been wiped out one night. How it had been effected was a mystery. Then a greater mystery. The commander of the town of Koropolis and twelve hundred of his men had simply vanished into thin air.

And in rapid order came the news of the disappearance of hundreds of thousands of Venusian warriors in scattered communities all over the United States. Strange stories began to circulate. Of odd-shaped vehicles that rolled with the speed of the wind, of men and women in dun-colored uniform that were impervious to the blasts of heat-pistols; of hidden arsenals and meeting places. And of a foursome, a man, a woman, a stranger from another planet and a bird that had the face of a man. These four were the leaders of the revolt against the bird-men.

For it was the bird-men who were the terrible people. They had no feelings. Emotion was something they did not possess. To kill was to their liking. Destruction was something to feed on. They were the real rulers. And their feet were heavy on the necks of the people of the

Earth.

Gundar knew the identity of the four.

He sat on his throne and brooded. Somehow he had to find them and exterminate them. He had in mind a special torture for Corono. It was he who was the prime factor in this revolt and resurrection. For resurrection it could surely be called. Men and women were no longer afraid to offer up their lives in the cause of freedom. It seemed as if the spirit of their forebears had suddenly come alive in their breasts.

Gundar projected his thoughts to the commander of a certain area:

"To the man or men who discover the whereabouts of these four I will offer a province and my protection. Larry Lipton, Gloria Kane, Corono, and Forgan.

"I will give the people of the Earth one week in which to disgorge them. Then I shall lay waste the land, kill off all the men-children, force the men into slavery and the women into bondage for my warriors and those of Venus. It is my command!"

DEEP IN the depths of the twisted ruins of what had once been the city of Chicago a vast community had been built. It lay underground in the vast installations that had once housed the water tunnels that supplied the city's twenty millions of people with water. Three million men, women and children lived in these vast tunnels.

And among them were Larry, Forgan, Corono and Gloria Kane.

Forty men and women were gathered about an immense circular table. At the head sat Larry and his friends. Larry waited until the last of his group commanders found a seat at the table. Then he arose and said:

"I think the time is at hand. It must be now before Gundar organizes, before we become too unwieldy for our work, and mostly before the spy organization he has set up becomes effective.

"Soon or late we will be found out. Because we have acted as guerrillas we have been successful. Now we must act as an army. The weapons, men and materials are enough for our purpose. The final plans must be discussed here and now."

A short stocky woman arose as Larry sat down. Her face bore the scars of a great sorrow. She had lost a man and three sons in the holocaust of war. She was known as Annie the Killer.

"Gundar has offered a province for the capture of our leaders. A province…" she turned and spat. "And if by the end of the week the traitors are not turned up he will do what has already been done.

"I like this Gundar. He is a man. A man with wings. The angels were said to have worn wings, I read of them. But this monster is an angel of death. He must be destroyed, he and all the lesser-winged monsters, and the grey hordes from Venus, I have spoken."

Another arose as the woman sat down. He was old, bent, and he leaned tiredly against the table edge. His face was wrinkled with age but his eyes were keen and his voice, though gentle, held vestiges of the power that once had been his. He had been the Vice-President of the United States.

"It is always good to hear the gentle Annie talk. She

never lets us forget the reason for our very existence. This is as it should be. But our wills and lives mean nothing. It is to the four who sit up there at the head of the table to whom we must look. It was their doing that has brought us to the heights we now occupy and lifted us from the depths of despair. So let them say what shall and will be done. Are we agreed?"

The forty voices rose as one in a shout of affirmation.

Larry looked to Corono, who nodded, stood and said:

"Good. And we are ready. There are fifty thousand of us here in the tunnels. Altogether there are two and a half million of us scattered the length and breadth of this land. And across the waters in other lands are another million. These must be coordinated. It is our plan."

When he finished the men and women seated about the large table looked into each other's eyes and smiled. The day would soon be when the land would be free and men could look men in the eye as they had in the past, and not with the furtive fear they had to show.

THERE WERE four hundred Venusian ships in the three triangles. They flew low on patrol. It was unusual that so many ships were used, but this was an unusual patrol. A spy had reported to the Indianapolis headquarters that a large concentration of men, machines and materials were near a large forest eighty miles from the city.

What the commander didn't know was that the spy who had done the reporting was a spy for Larry and the forty of his council.

The commander had sent up his entire fleet, three hundred fighters and a hundred bombers. They flew in three formations, with the bombers in the center triangle. If what the spy reported were true, the commander realized, he was made.

They flew low, secure in the knowledge that they were invulnerable. There had been not a single report of any antiaircraft fire. Not even a report that the enemy had such guns. As for ships, it was preposterous. Hadn't they wiped the Heavens free of them?

So they cruised back and forth over the area described by the spy. Lower and lower they flew and slower and slower did they throttle down until their speed was a hundred miles an hour. There were no gun flashes to warn them. They did not even see the guns.

It was over in five minutes, by Larry's watch. Not a ship of the entire four hundred remained in the sky. Larry knew, however, that some messages had gone through. But he was satisfied. What Corono had invented would make them impossible to find. Corono had found a means of making a cloth invisible to the naked eye. And with it glasses, which the Earthmen wore, that permitted them to see the huge section of cloth. The entire insides of the antiaircraft gun barrels were coated with the paint. They were impossible to see from a foot away.

It was the first important victory the Earthmen had over the combined forces of Gundar and his Venusian allies. Nor was it to be the last. The invisible paint that Corono had invented placed victory within their grasp.

But they reckoned without Gundar. He had a very good idea that the camouflage was paint. And that only a certain optical glass, colored in such a way and with only such a chemical that would permit the light beam to become visible, would be effective against it. He spurred his scientists toward that goal. They solved the puzzle eventually but not before Gundar and the Venusians had been driven out of all but their last stronghold.

The forces of the Earth were now on the march. There had been a gigantic upsurge of power. A government of the world had been proclaimed, the council of forty was the official voice of that body, and millions of soldiers had been enlisted and outfitted. Even the air force had been revived and refurnished with ships and guns. The great cities of the Earth had been put to use, plants had begun the manufacture of war materials and victory seemed in sight.

Then came the night of the 'message.'

It was a voice, a voice that had been heard in every corner of the world. The voice simply said, "I shall destroy the whole world if it does not lay down its arms. Furthermore, if the four arch-enemies are not placed in my hands within the next twenty-four hours, I will then make good my threat."

THE COUNCIL of forty were in session at the instant of the broadcast. It was as if Gundar knew they would be. Larry paled at the words and turned and looked at Corono.

"Would he...?" he couldn't finish what was on his mind.

"Yes. I think he would," Corono said. "And he has the means. I know because I gave it to him. Gundar is clever as a devil. He took into consideration the fact that perhaps all wouldn't go well. So he told me to make a weapon that would destroy this planet should he fail in his invasion plans.

"What is more, we can't stop him."

"But if you invented it why can't you invent something that would..."

Corono was shaking his head all the while Larry was talking. Larry stopped and waited for the other to say what he had to.

"It is only a pinch of powder," Corono said. "My greatest invention. It sets up a disturbance. Small at first, like the start of the whirlwind, it grows in intensity until the whole planet is involved in the mad whirling dance. And finally it spins out of control into space. Nothing can stop it once that pinch of powder is released. I do not have to say what happens to those on the surface of the planet, do I?"

There was no need to answer.

"So we've got twenty-four hours, eh?" a raucous voice demanded. "So let's get on the ball. What the hell? We ain't licked till the last man's out. And it's our turn at bat..."

It was the voice from the birdcage. Forgan's voice. The expression or the tiny gargoyle face as truculent as ever, the sneer in the voice dominant as the desire to live. Larry reached over, picked up the cage and said:

"I never thought the day would come when I'd want to kiss that double-ugly pan of yours. But it has. And if ever we can get you out of this wire gimmick, I'm going to do it, if I have to get punched in the nose for it."

"'S matter? Gettin' soft?" Forgan asked. But the wide grin took the sting from the words.

"Well, if he isn't," Gloria said, "I am. And if he doesn't keep his promise, I will for him."

"For that I'll wait," Forgan said.

But though the words were wonderful to listen to Corono wanted to know what was going to be done about it.

"There's only one thing we can do about it. Since Mohammed wants us to come to him, let's. Gloria did it several times. So have you and so have you. Maybe not to Gundar, but to others. It's just another place we haven't visited. How about it?"

"As Forgan would say, I'm game," Corono replied.

"All right, then. We've got twenty-four hours. Will Gundar give us another twenty-four hours?" Larry asked.

"If I know Gundar, he won't. His will is not the kind to be brooked. Further, he makes the decisions. He said twenty-four hours, and he meant just that. Whatever is on your mind will have to be accomplished in that period."

"Then here's what we do," Larry said. "Forgan will have to remain here, of course…sorry, pal," he broke into Forgan's objections, "…this is one time you're out of the picture. We can't take a chance dragging you along. The girl, Corono and myself will get into this Room of the King he built near Los Angeles. Here's how…"

CHAPTER SEVEN

THERE WAS a disturbance before the vast gates of the city walls.

The armed guards looked on in amusement. An unkempt beggar was screaming imprecations at the head of a cavalcade of motor-jet cars. The man beside the driver looked coldly at the beggar and tossed him a couple of coins and the mendicant bowed so low his broken nose seemed to touch the ground. Then the well-dressed man motioned for the sergeant of the guard to step close.

"I do not have a pass to enter," he said. "But if you will notify the King's chamberlain that I have Gloria Kane prisoner it will go well with you."

The mention of her name worked wonders. In a few moments the gate swung wide and the lead car and its three mates drove into the city of Los Angeles. Already there to meet it was an honor guard, with Savor at its head. He stopped the car with an imperious gesture and said:

"Who are you? And where is the woman?"

The man answered softly: "I am Jake Jones. And I like the color of a man's money. It's the only thing I have ever liked. See? The King wants to see the dame, nobody but the King gets to see her."

The grin was wiped from his lips at Savor's sudden gesture; a heat pistol thrust its unwavering muzzle into the man's belly.

"The girl," Savor demanded.

"In the third car," came the surly answer.

Savor's face bore a wild expression of triumph, as he peered into the darkened interior and looked into the eyes of Gloria Kane. "So. It is she. Gundar will give you more than just money, Mister Jones," Savor shouted. "He will make you a Prince. Come! To the palace…"

Nobody noticed that the beggar had flattened himself

along the wall and, as the last car went through, so did the beggar. Nor did anyone see that the man slipped from the rear of the last car as Savor was questioning the driver of the lead car.

The night was moonless. Not a soul walked the darkened streets. At least no one who saw the ragged beggar sidling along the curbstone, head bent as if he were looking for a dropped cigarette, or coin. It was a street of pretentious homes, semi-estates. It was the street on which Tom Heine lived. Suddenly the beggar walked over to the wall fronting the house and slumped against its pink stone. A cab pulled up before the house and a man got out. The man walked with a limp. A grey beard covered his lower lip and mouth. He paid the driver and limped toward the entrance. The beggar accosted him with open palm and the limping man dropped something into it. The beggar lurched off.

An hour later the same beggar was seated before the curb of a darkened door. The door bore letters that said there was a restaurant on the second floor. A cab stopped before the curb and two men got out. One limped, wore a beard and gold-rimmed spectacles. The second man was Tom Heine. Heine paid the driver and he and the limping man opened the door to the restaurant and walked in. And after a moment the beggar tried the door. It opened easily and the darkness swallowed him also.

"WE DID IT!" Larry shouted as obscure figures closed in on him. "We did it!"

Instinct made him strike even before he realized the figures he thought were Corono and Heine were not.

His fist sank into the soft belly of a man. Then the figures were on him, striking with clubs, with fists, pummeling him to the ground and finally into unconsciousness.

He opened his eyes and felt the dull stab of pain strike his eyeballs. He tried to repress the groan that came to his lips but it escaped him.

"Larry," a voice whispered. "Are you all right, boy?"

It was Tom Heine.

"I—I guess so," Larry replied. "But I wonder what they hit me with, the ring posts?"

"They got this Corono friend of yours and me before we could open our yaps. Damn! I wonder how they got wise?"

"Too late for that," Larry said. "Where are we?"

The darkness was complete. He could make out the dim outlines of a window, felt the embrace of walls, and knew he was bound. He rolled in the direction of Heine.

"Try these knots, Tom," he said. "Maybe I can do the same for you."

But they were knots fashioned from wire. It was no use trying to get free of those. Larry lay back and tried to figure out how it was they had been betrayed. Who could have done it and for what reason? It had to be someone in the council. It had been so simple. Gundar was not alone in having men spy for him. There were more who worked for Larry and the council of forty. That was how Tom had been contacted and how the elaborate masquerade was arranged. Now it was all over.

He gripped himself hard at the thought that had suddenly come to mind. What about Gloria? If they knew about Corono and Larry's disguise they also knew about the ruse that had allowed Gloria to get trapped. And where was Corono? What bit of terror had they in mind for him?

HE LIFTED his head as the door to the room opened and light streamed in. He saw the figure of a man outlined in the light. It was impossible to make out who the man was. But the huge shadow made the wings that folded back along the blades even more grotesque and fearsome than the man himself.

"My friend," a resonant voice proclaimed in pious horror. "How pitiful your state."

Gundar waited until Larry had spent himself in empty cursing. Amusement crept into his voice:

"Did you think Gundar would be fooled by these theatricals? Beggar's costume, an old fool for an accomplice. The business of Gloria's capture and a man who wears gold-rimmed glasses and walks with a limp. *Really*...

"But now the play is over and the musicians must receive their tokens of payment. Take this young fool to the room prepared for him. And leave the old one here."

A dozen men stepped forward and while some stood guard others lifted Larry up and carried him down the length of a hall and into a large, well-lighted room. Gundar followed. They undid the bonds of his legs and held him erect against a wall while they made him secure to one of a number of bolts that protruded their lengths from it.

But Larry had eyes only for the figure of a man who hung limply from one of the bolts. It was Corono. And someone had gone to work on him. The scientist was bare to the waist and blood poured in slow streams from the ribboned flesh, where either a whip or lash had shredded him.

"Oh… He is alive, if that is what is worrying you," Gundar said. "The flesh can take a terrific amount of punishment. As you will find out." He gestured suddenly with a beckoning finger. And three half-nude men stepped forward. They were squat creatures, with shaven skulls and thick, muscular bodies. Each carried a long-handled lash. Gundar smiled pleasantly, as he said, "Strip the clothes from this one."

Larry gulped as the lash whistled and struck. Fire raced down his chest. A streak of flame seared his shoulder, and another caught his right arm. He strained against the bonds until blood seeped from between the wires. Once more the three slashed at Larry and this drew what Gundar wanted to hear, a high whinny of pain and terror. Four more times the whips slashed and tore at him. They stopped then, only because he was no longer conscious to feel.

Gundar made a face of disgust. He spoke aloud, "Sad. Very sad that a man can no longer enjoy what was once his greatest pleasure. Perhaps the woman will renew my lease on life. I have my doubts on that score. These Earth people have no fire in their veins. Aah, well. Time will tell…"

"LARRY! LARRY!" a voice was calling him back from the land of the dead. He tried to open lids that seemed glued to each other. Again the urgent call. Oh, but it was so good to float on that unguent stream where the water ran so smoothly over one's naked body. There was only content in that wondrous tide. Once more the call. *Hang the man!* Why couldn't he let one alone?

Might as well open one's eyes and see who it is that calls. But this stickiness, this difficulty in prying them open by will alone. But of course. One had only to lift one's hand and use one's fingertips.

The scream that came from Larry Lipton's lips had the sound of insanity in it.

"Easy, Larry," Corono shouted. "Easy boy. We can't lose our senses now."

"Aah… Aah…" Larry sighed windily. "Oh, I feel as if I'd been bathed in fire. Whew. Aah, I can't take too much of that."

"I don't think we'll have to, Gundar tires quickly of everything. He didn't know it but I was awake when he gave his usual soliloquy. He won't bother us again until the time comes for our departure from this veil of tears.

"But before that time we must free ourselves. We must. He has Gloria in his power."

Larry steeled himself to think on a straight line, to forget this horrible pain that possessed every fibre of his being, which insisted on making itself felt at every second. Self-hypnosis. It was the only way. And after a while he forgot. He forgot because he willed himself to; there were other, more important things than himself to consider. But though he forgot his pain he could not think of a single way in which freedom could be obtained.

"You're right, pal," he said. "I'm trying to think. But it's no good. Gundar has us by the short hair."

Corono laughed shortly. "Perhaps after our bellies

are full. It is always easier to think on a full stomach."

"How do you know we are going to eat?" Larry asked, just to hear himself talk. His mind was on other thoughts.

"The thoughts of one of the guards were projected to me," Corono said.

"OHH, WHAT was that?" Larry's voice bristled with excitement.

"I said that I had received a mental image of one of the guard's thoughts."

"That's what I thought you said. Corono! I think we've got the answer. If you can get a mental picture of a thought, why can't you project one? Why can't you order the guard to release us?"

"Why—I had never thought of it in that light. But how simple it would be. Thought projection-command is a matter of superior mental powers. Wait... Let us see how well it works..."

A dozen men walked into the lighted room. They walked with the mechanical steps of automatons. While one of their number unlocked the bonds that held Corono and Larry to the wall the others waited stiff as stone statues. Then, at another voiceless command, they handed their arms to the two men.

"How long will they remain like that?" Larry asked as they stalked stealthily down the hall.

"So long as they receive no other command. But you have opened up a new field of control for me, Larry. And possibly a way to circumvent Gundar."

As one, they heard the marching sound of sandaled feet. They melted into a break in the wall, as if they had become shadows. A half dozen winged soldiers walked by and disappeared down the shadowed far end. Once more the two men advanced.

They came at length to a corridor that forked two ways, both at right angles to the main corridor. Corono held Larry's arm and closed his eyes. "Down this way," he said. "I opened my mind and received an impression of voices in this direction."

It was a hall of magnificent statuary, of wondrous paintings, of elegant furnishings and drapes. Not a soul disturbed the tranquility of the marble floor, not a breath of sound the quiet of its golden walls. Only a pair of shadows slipping along, taking advantage of every fold of drape, of every column that might hide one. And at the end a pair of huge doors, a hundred feet in height, blazing with the gems of an entire planet's sacking. The gate to the Room of the King.

Once more there was the sound of marching feet, but this time a great sound, as of many, many feet.

"In here," Larry whispered.

The crimson folds of a pair of magnificent silk drapes closed their beauty about the two men. And though they could not be seen, they could see. At the head of a long line of winged soldiers, Savor, his eyes set straightforward, his shoulders back stiff as always, marched. Larry stopped counting at a thousand. A wide grin was on Corono's lips when the last of the winged men marched through the open gates, which had swung wide to receive them, and had closed themselves after the last passed through.

"Larry," Corono said, as he stepped squarely before the huge doors, legs spread wide in an attitude of reckless abandon, his naked back and shoulders bearing the unhealed welts of the lashing he had gotten. Larry felt his breath catch at the magnificent display of bravado. This was a man. "This is it, Larry," Corono said, as he turned for a last look at Larry. Then his brow knit in terrific concentration. Larry felt sweat trickle down his eyes, as he tried to put himself in his friend's place.

And after a while the huge doors began to open, slowly...

CHAPTER EIGHT

GLORIA FELT the heat of shame sweep over her. Not even in the nude had she felt so naked, so much the cynosure of all eyes. A feeling of the deepest sadness overwhelmed her. Her lover, her friends, the greatness of their mission, all gone. Despair rode hard on her. How could they have thought themselves so clever as to imagine they could win out over this winged devil, Gundar?

She thought back to how he had received her. It was as if she were an insect under the impersonal gaze of a microscope. His eyes had looked her over as if she were something strange to him, a worm, an anything but human being. Then Gundar had smiled.

And that was even worse, for in his smile there was a promise. A promise he had made to himself on another world, a promise to discover what the opposite sex could mean to Gundar.

"Really, Miss Kane," he said. "All this buffoonery wasn't needed. This play of being captured and this elaborate business of being brought here. Mister Jones is receiving his reward. I promised it to the man who brought you here. And he shall get it, never fear. A province. The whole of an iceberg at the North Pole. He shall be chained to it forever, so that no one shall not know it is his. Is that not a fine reward?"

Gloria's head had come up. "The sort of reward a devil like you would think of," she had said in scathing tones.

Laughter had gone up at her words. Gundar's smile deepened. "My friends seem amused by you, Miss Kane. I wonder if their amusement will grow when I tell them you are to be my Empress?"

His evil eyes swept the length and breadth of the huge room. Not a soul dared look into those eyes. His mouth, sneered.

"Bah. Less than worms, I find you!" he lashed at them. "Take them away. The whole lot of them, Venusians and all."

He dismissed them on the instant nor did he look to see whether his orders were being carried out. Instead his eyes searched hers.

"They weary me with their fawning, sycophantic ways," he said. "And those clumsy louts, the Venusians. They think to kill a man is the supreme art... And so clumsy at it, so lacking in finesse. But they live but to die. How can they understand?

"Miss Kane. Your friends will soon be here to, as they hope, release you. The wires attached to your body. They will do you no good. Gundar is not taken in by such foolery. So make yourself at ease and allow your good judgment to hold sway. While there is life there is hope, it is said. Do not give up."

He was laughing at her. She knew it. His words about Larry and Corono. He knew of their whole plan. What was the use? She did not realize what she was doing. Her fingers swept up and aimed themselves at the side of her throat.

But they never reached their goal. It was as if she had become paralyzed. She could not move a muscle. Gundar stepped from the dais and moved to her side. His fingers slipped the wires from her hand and threw them to one side.

"Now, my dear," he said. "If you wish to play, there are better games than suicide."

He bent and pressed his lips to hers. For an instant surprise gripped her. Then her hand came up and slapped at him. The marks of her fingers were white against the suddenly scarlet skin as he stepped back.

"My dear," his voice was silky, "I have never kissed a woman. I know it is an Earthly custom. Is the slap part of the game?"

HE DID not wait for her answer. Instead, he turned to the winged warrior who served as his chamberlain and said, "Dress her as is the lowest of the courtesans and send her under escort to the barracks of the Venusian soldiers. She is to be their plaything until they tire of her. Then…" His shoulders shrugged and he turned and walked from her.

Now she looked at the filmy covering that served only to accentuate her charms and bowed her head. She was to be taken before Gundar first, so that he could look at her shame.

The winged chamberlain gestured with his head for her to follow him. And once more she was in the Room of the King. She saw that this time she was the only woman in the place. Fully a thousand men were crowded in the vast room. Yet so large was it, that when the doors swung wide and Savor marched in at the head of two thousand foot soldiers, not even they filled the place.

The chamberlain waited to one side. Gundar was busy in discussion with a gigantic Venusian. Whatever Gundar was saying did not sit well with the grey giant.

"No!" he shouted suddenly. "The men of Venus are not children to be bilked of their rightful spoils so easily, Gundar. Your promise must be kept."

Something in the Venusian's tone made Gundar look up in surprise. What was wrong with the man? They had been talking easily and to mutual agreement, and suddenly this shouting. Silence fell on the vast hall. The grey giants from the Silver Planet, Venus suddenly turned grim. Was something amiss?

"Now, Hag-U." Gundar tried to calm the other down. "You did not hear me aright."

Hag-U stepped back a pace, his hand low at his energy belt. "I heard you a right, Gundar!" he shouted. "Treacherous knave!"

The words were a signal for bedlam to let loose. In an instant every man in the vast room went berserk. The giant Venusians were skilled warriors, though Gundar made small of their ability. With the first shot they formed into small groups that went to make up a larger one, which in turn became the point of a triangle aimed straight at the dais.

And as more and more Venusians joined the small groups they gravitated toward the wide base of the triangle so that as some fell more would take their place.

The winged soldiers of Gundar took wing on the instant. The green flashes of heat energy filled the air and made the heat unbearable. On the dais Hag-U seemed frozen in the truculent attitude of hand on energy pistol. His lips grimaced in hate, his eyes gleamed, and his body was tense. But Hag-U was dead. Gundar had killed him with a single look.

But though Gundar's soldiers fought, Gundar was no longer there to see the outcome of the battle. He had whirled, seized Gloria and dragged her through the narrow archway of an anteroom. She tried to struggle against him, but he held her in a grip that was like steel. She even tried to drag herself against him, but he pulled her as if she weighed ounces, and after a while she moved swiftly behind him.

THE WAY was in gloom, the ceiling but a few feet above them. It was Gundar's passage to his aviary. He stopped before the doors and they swung open for him. And once more Gloria imagined herself back on that terrible planet from which they had escaped. The same birds chattering their twittering sounds.

Gundar threw her to a couch close by, while he sat deep within the sheltering arms of a large wing chair. His eyes were clouded in deep thought. His fingers tapped restlessly on the arms of the chair. Now and then the fingers of one hand came up to caress the chin.

"I don't understand," he said after a few moments time went by.

"I don't understand. It is as if someone *commanded* Hag-U to say what he did. His death is meaningless, I was tired of the boor, anyway. But this wild fray that is taking place. I don't understand it at all."

"Perhaps Gundar is losing his powers," Gloria taunted him. "Perhaps their strength is greater than yours...?"

He shook his head. "No. It is not that. I must reason it out. Be still, woman."

He kept shaking his head as if he could not bring his mind to an understanding of the situation. The solution came to him in a flash. "Hah! Someone *is* commanding them. Corono. He is the only one who has the power. Now we shall see..."

His eyes closed and a look of intense concentration came over his face.

THE GREAT gem-studded doors swung wide. Larry's reflexes came into instant play. He had glimpsed the huge grey bodies pressed close to the doors as they started to come open. His arm swept Corono into the protection of the great fold of drapes that hung alongside one of the sections. Then the thousands of fighting men swept out into the corridor. Men died and were trampled by others taking their place. Above, the winged men flew and darted down in swift dips to empty their heat pistols into the bodies of the Venusians. Larry saw that it was only a matter of a short time before the grey giants would be wiped out.

But the present was not the moment of the grey Venusians' defeat. They gave as good as they got and the battle swayed this way and that. Gundar's winged legion had but the weapons of their wings and their side arms. The Venusians carried short, wide swords with which they did devastating work at close quarters. And since a great part of the fight was at close quarters, the walls, drapes, statuary, floor, were soon covered by a slick coating of crimson.

It was the winged divers who decided the battle. Had it been man to man, or even pistol against pistol, the Venusians would have won out. But it wasn't. So in the end they were forced back down the length of the long corridor, back until the sound of the battle was a small echo in the ears of the men behind the folds of the drape.

"What now?" Larry asked.

"I don't know," Corono said hesitantly. "Gundar knows who forced this issue. *Stay close Larry.*" The last was said in a rush of words.

Corono stiffened suddenly. Sweat stained his face and gave it an oily appearance. Slowly, step by straining step, he moved through the wide-open gates, Larry close at his heels. Down the immense length of the Room of the King, Corono walked. His face was intense with concentrated mental strain. Larry could not speak. He knew a single word would break the tide of battle in Gundar's favor. And without being told, he knew Gundar had established contact with Corono.

It was the last battle, the end for one of the two, and possibly the end for all the Earth people.

The look of strain departed, though sweat still poured in steady streams from Corono's features. He was no longer tense. But it wasn't because the issue had been decided in his favor. It was only the state of mind he had placed himself in. A complete forgetfulness of surroundings.

YEARS SEEMED to pass as the two men walked slowly, laboriously; it was evident Corono did not want to meet Gundar face to face. The narrow archway seemed an interminable distance. Yet it was only a matter of moments altogether, and they stood framed in the arch. Then they were through.

Corono's guttural breathing was the only sound in the stillness of the covered areaway. Larry's breath came in slow, shallow gasps, audible only to himself, like the slow, steady pounding of his heart. Then the narrow door confronted them. As if by its volition, it swung wide and the two men stepped over the threshold.

Instantly, the spell was broken for Larry.

He was back on the planet from which the invasion had begun. It was the room of the birds again. They perched on their bars, tier on tier of them, swinging gently to and fro, millions of them, tiny symbols of Gundar's power. Their voices were still. Yet Larry had the odd impression their eyes were intent on the mental battle going on below them.

He looked up and up at them, to where the last row perched on a swinging bar fully two hundred feet from the floor. A wild thought came to him. A man's mind had placed them in their present voiceless form because he had feared, or hated, or simply because some had incurred his displeasure. Perhaps it would only take another's mental effort to free them?

He turned quickly to see how Corono was doing. And saw Gloria for the first time. He gulped at the sight of her lovely body, so captivatingly displayed in the flimsy bits of lace network Gundar had forced her to wear. Her eyes met his for a second and in them he read for the first time the love she bore him. Yet he could not go to her, despite the sudden ache his arms developed for her. First Gundar's will had to be broken.

The stillness deepened until the silence was unbearable. There was menace and fear and terror in it. Even the birds seemed to feel it. They left their perches and flew aimlessly, silently about, and not even the flutter of the countless wings gave sound to the electric air.

There was only the slow slithering of Corono's feet as he advanced straight for Gundar.

Gundar was still seated in his chair. He seemed completely relaxed. No sweat stained his face, no strain narrowed his eyes. He seemed, in fact, to stare with complete abstraction at Corono, as if he were amused by the incident. Then Larry's eyes fell to Gundar's fingers on the arms of the chair, and the hope that had died when Corono mentioned Gundar was aware of the cause of the battle was renewed. It was only on the surface that Gundar was relaxed. Corono's will was thus far a match for his own.

As if Gundar was conscious of it, he said:

"Well done, Corono. I created you too well in my own image. But remember… *I* am the creator, and the destroyer, too."

For the smallest instant Corono's attention was diverted. And in that second Gundar acted. He stood swiftly, with a fluid motion that was like water. He took a single step forward and stared deeply, intently into

Corono's eyes. And this time there was no doubt of the effort he was putting out.

Larry became aware of the ticking of his wristwatch. The sound was maddening. Each second ticked off the approach of doom. Corono was going to lose this battle of hypnosis. Larry *knew* it. Something had to be done. He looked wildly about him. He had forgotten completely the heat pistol in his hand. He wanted only some familiar thing, a club, a knife, something with which to strike that haughty evil face, to make the monster tear his eyes away from Corono's.

BUT OF A sudden Larry was powerless to move. As if Gundar had read his mind, he chained Larry to immobility.

But not Larry's voice. Those wildly fluttering wings had given him an idea.

"The birds!" Larry shouted. "They hate Gundar."

And as Gundar's words had broken the concentrated effort of Corono, so did Larry's break that of Gundar. He looked away for one startled instant. And in that instant Corono sent a thought winging its way into the breasts of the closest perch.

Like a myriad of tiny arrows the birds dove straight down at Gundar.

But swift as was their action, even more swift was his. Whirling, he dove for the door to his left, and as he moved with a speed too great to intercept, he grabbed up Gloria under one arm.

Larry threw an arm out to stop him: Gundar's hold on him was broken the instant the birds were released, but Gundar crashed a stone-hard fist into Larry's face, knocking him to the floor. Larry heard Corono's voice as from a long distance.

"…There are too many of you. Perch by perch— So! That is better…"

Larry lifted himself from the floor and made for the door through which Gundar had escaped. He had seen what Corono was doing. But he had a single thought in his mind, Gundar had Gloria!

"Wait, Larry!" Corono shouted as he dashed after his friend.

The passage on which the door opened was dark and damp. Bare stone lined it and moisture was exuded from the pores of the rocks. Like some wild thing in pursuit of another, Larry ran, and behind him came Corono. The way was long. But the sound of Gundar's pounding feet ahead lent wings to Larry's own. Gundar was hindered by the weight of the girl. Larry was only a few feet behind the two when they broke into the open.

They were on a large, square of open space. Below, to the right, was the swelling, cream-capped Pacific. The thunderous sound of surf breaking on jagged rocks was loud in his ears. To the left, and extending for a hundred miles, were the myriad lights of Los Angeles. But Larry took all that in with part of his mind. His whole being was focused on the winged figure of the man in whose arms a lovely half-nude girl lay.

With a gesture of contempt, Gundar tossed the girl from him. She fell and lay still, as if in death. But the heaving of the snow-white breasts gave the lie to that. A wild laugh came from Larry's lips.

"So it's going to be man to man?" he said. "Or are you frightened of man to man?"

Suddenly Gundar's wings opened wide. They spread a full ten feet each way from his shoulder blades. "You see how easily I could have escaped," Gundar said softly. "But first I must remove a blot, a stain from my mind. And I must do it physically, because I made the mistake of allowing a physical contact by you Earthworms. Come to me, my friend, come to this warm embrace."

LIKE A TACKLER diving for the man with the ball, so did Larry dive at Gundar. And Gundar met him with a slashing swipe of his forearm. Larry skidded across the smooth stone to land against the waist-high parapet. He arose, shaking himself as he did, and came forward, arms and hands in a fighter's pose.

Gundar waited until Larry was a few feet off, then stepped in. Larry feinted, and Gundar made no move to protect himself. Then Larry threw a straight right into the other's face. The blow landed and Gundar staggered back. A thin stream of blood poured from one of Gundar's nostrils. He felt of it and held his fingers in front of him, a look of intense surprise on his face, as if he never seen his own blood before.

But Larry didn't wait to see what Gundar's reaction to that was going to be. His fists shot out like the strokes of a trip hammer, and slashed and hooked at the hated, evil features before him. Gundar fell back before the wild savage blows. Now he was bleeding from both nostrils and from a cut over the eye, and a lump appeared on the flesh below the left cheekbone.

Larry followed the retreating body relentlessly, driving his fists home hard, trying for the knockout punch.

Then Gundar struck. Only once, too swiftly for

human body to avoid. Larry took the clumsy blow on his left shoulder. Had it been in the face it would have smashed flesh and bone to pulp. The punch lifted him in an arc, to land in a skidding heap fully twenty feet away. Larry lifted himself by sheer power. His shoulder was numb and his arm hung limp at his side. But he still had his Sunday punch to throw, and he always used his right arm for that.

Even his brain was numb. He knew only that he had to smash that evil leering face to shreds. There was someone shouting to him, a voice that was familiar, but he could not attend to words. Not while Gundar was still standing.

But Gundar was no longer standing still. He came forward at a run.

"Now you will die!" Gundar shouted. "You have profaned my body. Death is the payment for that!"

Larry tried to leap aside, tried to duck the outthrust arms. But they enfolded him in a grip that was like a pair of steel bands. He felt himself lifted on high. He could see the rush of waters below, could hear their breaking on the saw-toothed rocks, and he felt himself fall...

HE ROLLED over and saw a strange thing. Gundar was being lifted on high by a dozen birds of such size as Larry had never imagined existed. They were fully twenty feet from back to tail-tip. Straight up the birds bore Gundar and then to one side. When they released him Gundar fell like a plummeting stone, and after him the wings, torn from the living flesh of his shoulder blades. Larry heard and shuddered at the pulpy sound the body made as it struck the rocks a thousand feet below.

Then Gloria was in his arms, a shuddering, whimpering Gloria, almost wild with hysteria that was at the very edge of her fingertips, on the tip of her tongue. Larry caressed the fear and fright away with gentle words and stroking fingers until the shudders left her, and her eyes looked up at him with love.

Corono cleared his throat. Startled, the two looked at him. There was a shy grin on the scientist's lips.

"Don't you think there is a time and place for that?" he said.

"Yes," Larry replied. "And the first thing we're going to do is find it. But first we've got to get to a preacher. There are a few words we have to hear."

Corono looked blank. Larry explained quickly, as they made their way back to the aviary.

"...And I guess it'll be the first wedding attended by two best men," he said in closing.

But he was wrong. At least insofar as time was concerned. There were many things that had to be attended to first. And many things explained. Gundar's death brought many problems. There were an immense number of men and birds to be released from their bondage. Corono had only released a few hundred, a dozen of which had come to Larry's rescue. All this took time.

But in the end it was done. And one night the greatest and strangest wedding in all history took place. It was attended by a half million birds of monstrous size, from whose lips came the most thrilling music ever heard. The wedding was tele-cast by the groom's best man, or rather one of them. The second stood at his side. And five billion people saw the telecast.

Corono stepped to Forgan's side after the wedding. The two men—the first thing Corono had done on their return was change Forgan back to his human form again—watched the honeymoon ship take off.

"Y'know, pal," Forgan said. "Pretty-puss wasn't a bad guy."

"No, he wasn't," Corono said. A sigh escaped him.

"What's wrong, pal?" Forgan asked.

"Strange, but in all the time I've been on this Earth, there has been one thought in my mind. To see a ball game. But always something prevented it."

"Well, pal," Forgan said gleefully. "Let's go. Them Bums is playing. And what bums they is…"

THE END

If you've enjoyed this book, you will not want to miss these terrific titles...

ARMCHAIR SCI-FI & HORROR DOUBLE NOVELS, $12.95 each

D-71 **THE DEEP END** by Gregory Luce
TO WATCH BY NIGHT by Robert Moore Williams

D-72 **SWORDSMAN OF LOST TERRA** by Poul Anderson
PLANET OF GHOSTS by David V. Reed

D-73 **MOON OF BATTLE** by J. J. Allerton
THE MUTANT WEAPON by Murray Leinster

D-74 **OLD SPACEMEN NEVER DIE!** John Jakes
RETURN TO EARTH by Bryan Berry

D-75 **THE THING FROM UNDERNEATH** by Milton Lesser
OPERATION INTERSTELLAR by George O. Smith

D-76 **THE BURNING WORLD** by Algis Budrys
FOREVER IS TOO LONG by Chester S. Geier

D-77 **THE COSMIC JUNKMAN** by Rog Phillips
THE ULTIMATE WEAPON by John W. Campbell

D-78 **THE TIES OF EARTH** by James H. Schmitz
CUE FOR QUIET by Thomas L. Sherred

D-79 **SECRET OF THE MARTIANS** by Paul W. Fairman
THE VARIABLE MAN by Philip K. Dick

D-80 **THE GREEN GIRL** by Jack Williamson
THE ROBOT PERIL by Don Wilcox

ARMCHAIR SCIENCE FICTION CLASSICS, $12.95 each

C-25 **THE STAR KINGS**
by Edmond Hamilton

C-26 **NOT IN SOLITUDE**
by Kenneth Gantz

C-32 **PROMETHEUS II**
by S. J. Byrne

ARMCHAIR SCI-FI & HORROR GEMS SERIES, $12.95 each

G-7 **SCIENCE FICTION GEMS, Vol. Four**
Jack Sharkey and others

G-8 **HORROR GEMS, Vol. Four**
Seabury Quinn and others